# TRAIN WRECK

LIFE SUCKS #1

ELISE FABER

TRAIN WRECK
by Elise Faber
Copyright © 2017 Elise Faber
Newsletter sign-up

TRAIN WRECK
Copyright © 2017 Elise Faber
Print ISBN: 978-1-946140-12-8
eBook ISBN: 978-1-946140-01-2
Cover Art by Jena Brignola

# LIFE SUCKS SERIES

***Life Sucks Series***
Train Wreck
Hot Mess
Dumpster Fire
Clusterf*@k
FUBAR
Perfect Storm
Free Fall

*Hubs,*
*I love you.*
*Thanks for never calling me a train wreck . . . even when I felt like one.*

# TRAIN WRECK

## NOUN

1. a chaotic or disastrous situation
2. a person whom disaster follows at every *freaking* turn
3. someone who could create disaster out of even the most innocuous situations
4. Pepper O'Brien

# ONE
## HUMAN DIRECTIONAL ADVERTISING

Pepper

"SO WHAT DO I DO EXACTLY?" Pepper asked, fumbling to hold the arrow-shaped sign as she wrestled her long red hair into a ponytail.

Bert, the owner and namesake of Bert's Burgers, gave an exaggerated sigh. "You stand on the corner. You hold the sign and maybe dance a little."

She should have brought a hat.

Her pale skin didn't like the sun, and Pepper knew she'd be one giant freckle in less than an hour. But she wasn't a complainer, so instead of running screaming out the door when her mind churned up the memories of the last time she'd danced —an Academy award-winning actor, blood, and her resultant flight from Plastic-town, USA—she nodded. "Got it."

Broken vases, expensive flowers crushed on the floor, armies of lawyers, publicists, and handlers were all in the past.

She'd been pigeonholed by her family's expectations for too long. This was her chance to slip out of the spotlight and have a slice of normalcy.

She gave Bert a bright smile and pushed through the door.

She needed this job.

Not just for the money. Her father would give her anything she asked for. In fact, after paying the settlement to Christian Strand—aforementioned Oscar-winning actor she'd almost managed to de-brain with his own award—her father had technically given enough for three lifetimes.

But she was tired of being her family's train wreck. Tired of being the thing her father threw money at even as he discounted her worth on every other level.

*Oh dear, poor Pepper crashed a Ferrari and destroyed an entire film set. She's such a mess, but hey, at least the movie is in the news.*

*That Pepper! She set fire to her dormitory at UCLA, and the entire building had to be evacuated when she attempted to cook a special dinner for her boyfriend. But, hey, the latest O'Brien film is set on a university campus—we can spin this.*

*Sigh. Pepper tried to set her class goldfish free by flushing it down the toilet and ended up scarring her classmates' delicate little psyches. But, hey, all drains lead to the ocean, right? O'Brien Films is producing a set-at-sea drama. We'll donate to clean water causes, drum up some positive publicity.*

"Ouch," she muttered when the door shut on her before she and the arrow had cleared it.

Pepper shoved the metal and glass panel back, wrestled her way through, and—

*Le sigh.*

Her talent wasn't in traditional interviews and social media posts, not like her brother. *He* was brilliant at lining up A-list celebrities, at getting features on the Today Show. She, on the other hand, was golden because of her screw-ups.

Everyone's favorite joke.

A bumbling fool with a sweet face and disposition. The girl

who everyone loved to laugh at, to exclaim that being born with the proverbial silver spoon didn't give a person everything.

She tripped on a crack in the sidewalk and nearly broke the cardboard sign in half.

Case in point, that silver spoon hadn't given her grace.

Hollywood might as well pat her on the head like a puppy.

*"Good girl, Pepper."*

*"Just stay in the news. The new movie releases next week."*

*"Keep messing up. Just make sure that your screw-ups are hilarious and relatable."*

She huffed inwardly. The chatter was enough to make a grown woman insane.

But this, being here, making it on her own was her chance to prove she could do *something* and not screw it up.

She would *not* screw this up.

"Pepper!"

Bert's head popped through the door—crazy white hair, bushy eyebrows, thick lumberjack mustache, and all.

"Yes?" She straightened her shoulders and tried to appear competent at . . . holding a sign.

"Right side up, please." The door clanged closed as she glanced down.

Hastily, she flipped the arrow so the text—"Cheeseburger, fries, and a drink! Only $6.99!"—was readable to most normal human beings. Her cheeks were hot. "Okay," she muttered to herself. "Not the best start, but it can only get better from here."

She ignored her inner voice, the one that was practically screaming she'd just jinxed herself.

*Enough.*

After popping in her earbuds, Pepper stepped near the curb and began to make the sign do a jaunty dance, white-girl rhythm be damned.

She stood in the shade from one of the mature trees lining

either side of the quaint Craftsman storefronts of Stoneybrook's downtown area. The city had recently undergone a refurbishment to make even the most casual of its shops and restaurants—specifically Bert's Burgers—appear sophisticated.

Cobblestone-covered walls and bright white wood columns gave the buildings a refined feel, and even the flowers filling each window box deemed it necessary to show off their brightest and prettiest blooms.

Her father had been the producer of a movie shot in the area several years before, and that income for the town had made the freshening up possible, not that she'd mentioned the fact to Bert.

She was trying to fly under the radar, not draw more attention to herself.

Pepper had enjoyed visiting before the restoration—a small town feel wasn't exactly common in Los Angeles—but even cleaned up, Stoneybrook still felt friendly, welcoming, and . . . refreshingly wonderful.

No one recognized her here. Paparazzi weren't waiting in the wings for her to screw up. Just blissful anonymity.

And a job to do.

Cars whooshed by as she bobbed around. Downtown Stoneybrook was busy at lunchtime, pedestrians enjoying the mild weather with a stroll along the slate sidewalks, and diners eating on the various restaurants' patios, each enclosed by ornate, wrought iron fencing.

A little shaky-shaky to the left, some wiggles to the right and, *crap*, almost taking out a group of businessmen striding down the tree-lined sidewalk.

Thankfully, they were faster than they appeared and dodged the arrow's point just in time.

"Sorry!" she called, straightening her Bert's Burgers' T-shirt and flashing her best smile before continuing her *advertising specialist* duties, which had been the actual title in the listing for the sign-holding job.

That was Internet job hunting for ya.

For a while it actually seemed like she was going to rock it. She bounced on the corner, didn't hit anyone, and only dropped the arrow a few times. Nobody seemed to be paying her much attention.

Despite promotion being the purpose of her job, she considered that a good thing.

No attention meant no disasters.

"I can totally do this," she said to herself, twirling the bright yellow and black sign. She could get through one day's work and not create a catastrophe.

A shriek pierced straight through the pop song blaring in her earbuds.

Pepper frowned.

Really, her dancing was not *that* bad.

Which was the precise moment she looked up and saw the car careening toward her.

*Move!*

But she couldn't. Her feet might as well have been glued to the ground. Stupidly, she watched as time slid forward in slow motion and the car came closer.

She could feel the vibration of the engine, its heat on her face. Her fingers ached from where she clenched the sign like some sort of shield.

The impact took her breath away.

## TWO
# FATE CAN BE A REAL BITCH
# SOMETIMES

PEPPER WAS PINNED to the ground.

Except it wasn't two tons of metal pressing her to the concrete. Instead, a hard, heavy—she sniffed and caught the spicy scent of sandalwood—*male* body was atop her.

"Are you all right?" the man asked as he leaned back.

She saw his face and frowned, something familiar about his features. A five o'clock shadow on a strong jaw, a narrow nose, a top lip just slightly larger than the bottom.

"Hey," he murmured. "Did you hit your—?"

That voice. Smooth as velvet with the hint of roughness beneath. The glimpse of a dimple. No. Make that *two* dimples. Caribbean blue eyes, a scar across his right brow—

A scar *she'd* put there during a childhood baseball game gone wrong.

"Son of a bacon bit!"

It was Derek.

*Derek* had saved her.

As in, handsome-as-sin, her *brother's* friend, Derek. As in the boy who'd seen her grow up, creating disaster in every possible moment, who'd ignored the monster crush she had on him, who'd never laughed, who'd looked on with compassion—

And pity.

Pepper couldn't forget the pity. That had squashed the crush right out of her.

She had *some* pride after all.

Derek shifted on top of her. "Umm. I'm all for bacon and bits, I guess?" A flash of those dimples. "But are you okay? Did you hit your head?" he asked. Apparently, it was small potatoes to have saved a woman from being crushed to death.

Unfortunately, aside from that general concern, there wasn't a slice of recognition in sight.

Couldn't he have gotten uglier in the five years since she'd seen him?

If fate was kind, Derek would have gone bald. Or maybe gained a pouch, one of those jiggly tires around the middle that were prevalent on her father's producer friends.

Instead, he was long and lean and—she shuddered, her heart going all squiggly—rock-hard muscle.

Life really sucked sometimes.

"I'm okay," she said, and if her voice was breathless it was because she'd just been tackled to the ground after almost being run over by a car, not because Derek was poised over her, his mouth inches from hers.

Not. At. All.

Okay, it was totally because he was on top of her. Because—putting her bacon bits and attempts to stifle her cursing aside—he was still the hottest fucking man she'd ever seen.

Jet-black hair. Pale blue eyes. A square jaw, lush lips, and dimples. The man had honest-to-God dimples.

How was that fair?

"Did you hit your head?" he asked again. His fingers were

already in her hair, one large hand having cradled her skull from impact.

He was a superhero, a phenomenon, a melter of hearts—

Or rather, of panties.

Pepper couldn't forget those, not when hers wanted to slide down her thighs and shoot off her feet. Not when she'd witnessed firsthand the parade of girls through his life.

"No." She shifted, wincing when her hair tangled on his fingers. "My head feels fine."

"Hang on," he said, smiling and making her heart actually skip a beat. Deftly, he extracted his hand and placed it on the ground near her shoulder. "I'm glad you're not hurt." He paused and tilted his head to the side. "I know this sounds like a pickup line, but you actually look familiar. Do I know you?"

"You're Derek," she murmured, adding when his brows raised in surprise but not recognition, "You went to school with my brother. Paul."

Her brother's name was enough, though, and to her disappointment, Derek pushed himself back and stood. Immediately, she missed the weight of him, the heat, the spicy scent. "You're not Paul's *little* sister?"

He took a step away from her, eyes darting from side to side, panic clouding his expression.

Awesome.

She'd had her fair share—okay *more* than her fair share—of disasters, but a man had never looked at her like she was the plague.

Okay, that wasn't true, either.

She'd just never had a man as hot as *Derek* react that way.

Not true either.

*Ugh*. Why couldn't her inner monologue give her a break?

Unfortunately, that wasn't her style and, truth was, she'd

never cared when men avoided her. But Derek was different. He had *always* been different.

She sighed. Because he'd always meant more.

"Yup," she said, forcing a smile and carefully sitting up. "Paul is my older brother."

Sirens blared in the background, steadily coming closer, and Pepper realized that a crowd had formed around them. People stared at her and yet, instead of wearing the usual disappointed expressions from home—bummed that her latest entertaining disaster was over—they all seemed concerned.

Concern aside, it was strange to not be responsible for the current predicament.

Well, at least not responsible for the car adorning the sidewalk like a seriously messed-up art project. Although, Pepper *had* been standing on the street corner with cars cruising by, and with her danger-magnet being extra powerful, she should have known better than to tempt fate.

Still—her gaze flicked around the gathered crowd—it was really bizarre to not have a dozen cell phones pointed in her direction, recording every moment of her latest screw-up.

"Pepper." Derek crouched down next to her, drawing her focus. "It really *is* you."

She tried to keep her words light, but they sounded tired anyway. "I'm still me."

"Wow." Derek blinked at her for another moment before grabbing her hand and helping her to her feet. He frowned as he stared at her palms. She glanced down and was surprised to see large scrapes covering the surface.

Not that she was feeling them.

Adrenaline, from both the car and Derek, had begun to hit her hard. She wasn't in any pain, but she was shaking. Or rather, trembling.

"I think—" Pepper stumbled. "I think I need to sit down."

Without preamble, Derek scooped her up into his arms and began walking. She glanced over his shoulder as they passed the car that was perched haphazardly on the sidewalk. Steam snaked out from under the hood and the engine made a horrible hissing noise. Worse was the arrow sign, which lay shredded beneath one wheel.

This wasn't her fault, but Pepper had the feeling she was so getting fired.

Two men had opened the driver's side door and were helping an elderly woman from the car. She had a cut along her forehead and blood had stained a large portion of her white hair.

Pepper shuddered.

"I was just trying to read the sign," the older woman said in a feeble voice. "It seemed like such a good deal."

"Don't look," Derek said, shifting her so she couldn't see the blood. Instantly, her stomach settled. "You're safe now."

Pepper certainly *felt* safe wrapped up in his arms.

Which wasn't the point.

"I just stood there like an idiot. Frozen." Her teeth chattered, and she ground them together to try to stop the vibration.

Derek shrugged, making her body press tighter against his chest. She was the dumbbell to his biceps curl.

Not a bad place to be, all things considered.

"Fight or flight," he said, and then his lips curved up slightly, revealing another flash of those devastating dimples.

Pepper actually felt her heart skip a beat.

Until he spoke again, and she had to wonder if all his DNA had gone into forming those little hollows rather than brain power.

"You chose to fight."

Her breath came out in a little rush. "I was planning on

fighting the car?" she asked incredulously. Yeah, not so much. She'd been stuck in place, frozen in inaction. "That's— you've lost it."

Derek chuckled and bent to set her on a bench. "Insults. That's better."

A frown pulled her brows together. Men. She didn't understand them. "You're not making any sense."

"Maybe," he said and tucked a strand of hair behind her ear. "But at least you don't look like you're about to pass out anymore." A beat. "Plus, there's plenty of time to berate yourself for *not* moving later."

Okay, truth was, he *had* distracted her. The dizziness had gone, her head had cleared. Not that she was going to tell Derek that. His confidence was a tangible thing radiating in the space around her. She didn't need to add fodder to his ego.

"So you're suggesting my subconscious was telling me I could take on that car?" She rolled her eyes. "With what? My hidden superhero powers?"

"I could see you punching down its hood then casually tossing the crumpled car to the side." He sat next to her, considering expression on his face. "I seem to remember you being like a force of nature when I used to visit your brother." He paused, gaze sliding down her body in a long, slow circuit before returning his mischievous blue eyes to hers. "Though you look a little different now."

Pepper snorted. "Boobs will do that to a girl. And I'm not *much* different"—she flicked a hand in the direction of her scalp —"not with this fire-engine red hair."

The conversation was helping to get rid of the hormones flooding her body—or at least the adrenaline—so she was no longer trembling. Of course, she was also aware of Derek with every single cell in her body, but that was a problem for a completely different day.

He tugged the end of her ponytail. "I could never forget this hair." A beat. "So what are you doing in Stoneybrook?"

Now wasn't *that* the question of the hour?

## THREE
## IT'S ALL IN A NAME

"PEPPER *O'BRIEN?*" Bert exclaimed. "I can't have an O'Brien working for me."

"You already have an O'Brien working for you," she pointed out. "And really, it's actually been a nice change of pace. It was —" Clamping her mouth closed before she could declare nearly getting run over by a car *fun,* Pepper gave Bert a pleading look. "Give me another chance." Her eyes flicked out the front windows of the restaurant. No less than three police cars and two motorcycles surrounded the scene of the accident.

Flashing lights. Pedestrians milling about, clustering into groups, chatting.

If this had been Hollywood, tongues would already be wagging and rumors flying.

Pretty soon the gossips would have had Pepper playing chicken with cars and purposefully causing accidents left and right.

"It's not about chances." Bert shook his head. "Look, you seem like a nice girl, but your father is—"

Just a typical workaholic dad, she wanted to say.

She didn't.

Because he wasn't.

And also because O'Briens didn't air their dirty laundry . . . not unless it sold movie tickets.

Forcing a smile, Pepper said, "I understand." She hesitated. "Do you know anyone else who might be looking for . . ."

She trailed off, the "someone like me" unsaid.

Bert grimaced. "I believe Rose's Flower Emporium is looking for an investor."

"Ah," she said, eyes sliding closed. "Thanks." And with a heart that felt significantly heavier than it had several hours before, Pepper walked from the restaurant.

Derek was waiting for her.

He'd taken his turn to talk with the police after she'd given her statement, and despite the happy dance her heart broke into at the sight of all his gorgeousness, she had been hoping Derek would have gone back to whatever ridiculously sexy hole he'd crawled out of.

Wishes, rainbows, unicorns. So much nonsense.

She sighed.

"Let me give you a ride home," he said, pushing off the wall he'd been leaning on and crossing over to her.

"I'm fine."

"You're limping."

"I'm *used* to limping." Not that she was about to admit her ankle hurt.

"Well, *I'm* used to driving." Derek smiled and it melted her insides into goo she futilely tried to keep in place. But it oozed through her fingers, warmed her tummy. Lower.

Pepper tripped.

It was pure chance that she managed to right herself before her face met pavement. That and Derek snagging her arm to steady her.

A barely withheld groan. She was so tired of looking like an idiot.

Correction: she was *especially* tired of looking like an idiot in front of Derek today.

With a series of inner curse words that would have certainly gotten her a lead story on the gossip columns, Pepper yanked free and took off down the sidewalk.

"I'm also used to driving," he added, hurrying to catch up when she turned the corner and headed for the beach. "Particularly when my best friend's sister has nearly been run over."

Her rented cottage was less than a mile away and backed up to a public stretch of oceanfront. All cool breezes, salt-tinged air, and white sand everywhere.

She loved it.

Which is why Pepper wanted to be home. *Alone*. In bed. With a book and a gallon of wine.

But when Derek merely kept pace with her, she couldn't stop herself from continuing the banter. "You rescue best friends' sisters from being crushed by cars often, then?"

"At least once a week."

Dimple alert.

An idiot-inducing double dimple alert as Derek unleashed the full force of his megawatt smile on her.

Pepper concentrated her remaining functioning brain cells on navigating the street. She'd been reared amongst Hollywood's finest and should be immune to all forms of masculine presence. Unfortunately, her brain and body had never gotten on board with ignoring the yumminess that was Derek.

"Hey," he said, breaking into the jumble of her swirling emotions by wrapping his hand around her arm and tugging her to a stop. "I thought we were doing pretty good on the whole I-talk-then-you-talk thing."

Pepper glanced up.

Then wished she hadn't. Because Derek was staring down at her, eyes gentle, and—*hell no*—they couldn't have that.

The only reason she hadn't been shredded to a pulp in her teenaged years was because he'd barely acknowledged her existence. This—being charming and sweet, shit, one might even say *flirting*—and she'd crumple like a cheap ass suitcase under the weight of Derek's . . . well, his Derek-ness.

She'd watched many a girl stronger than her fall. Painfully.

"Got it. You're an expert damsel-in-distress rescuer," she said, her tone mild—though much more mild than she wanted. She wanted to be cold, closed off, damn near acerbic. "So there's that. Kudos to you."

"Hey. *Hey*. Slow down." He caught her arm again. "Let me at least walk you where you're going, Pep."

"My name is *Pepper*," she snapped before catching herself and forcing a lighter tone, because reacting to that nickname gave too much away, gave too much power over her past, her family. She'd moved to Stoneybrooke because she wanted to get away from all of that, not because she wanted to bathe in the memories. "Or Ms. O'Brien," she said, lips curved. "Or even 'Hey you,' but it most certainly isn't *Pep*."

His eyes locked on hers, searching intently. Pepper's gut twisted because that look seemed to tell her that Derek could see straight through her, through the lightness. He lifted a brow. "This not liking the name Pep—is it a recent development?"

*Fuck.*

"No," she said after a moment. "I've always hated it." Then started walking again.

Because, enough already.

Andy, her ex, had called her Pep and since she wasn't talking or thinking about her ex-fiancé—who'd had an affinity for anyone in panties that wasn't her—there wasn't any point in discussing it. She'd broken things off after discovering what he'd done, but it still hurt. She'd loved the jerk, and he'd thrown that aside for a few orgasms.

Derek followed her down the sidewalk.

Ugh.

But then their feet scuffed against the sand scattered along this stretch of pavement, the sounds of the ocean beginning to overpower those of Stoneybrook's downtown.

Home was close.

"Why don't you like it?" he asked softly.

"It's not me." That she'd answered him surprised her. Usually she played off the nickname, despite not liking it. Not wanting to make a fuss over some silly teasing when Pepper made enough of a fuss in her wake.

But, truth was, she hated that stupid epithet with a vengeance. It was too cheerful. Too carefree. Too much lightness and not enough calamity.

Derek shoved his hands into his pockets and blew out a breath. "And the reason you never said anything was?"

"It didn't really matter." A pause. "And Andy seemed to like it." She shrugged, determinedly pushing all thoughts of Andy the asshole and how she'd been with him away. "I never expected it to stick. Plus, Paul thought it was fitting. He always said I've got pep in my—"

"Step," Derek said. "I remember. Because you were always so happy."

His tone was so gentle that, for a moment, Pepper's eyes stung. But she blinked the tears away as she did everything else.

With sheer determination.

Happy. Yeah, not exactly.

"Happy," she murmured, "how could an O'Brien be anything but?"

She'd had a fiancé from an important family, a father who spent loads of money on her, and . . . that was just it exactly. She had what? Not a career. Not anything to claim as her own. She would never be anything more than a flighty daughter or wife.

Which was most of why she'd called off her engagement.

The other, of course, being that Andy had been screwing his assistant. Or rather *assistants.*

Her feet stopped moving. Pepper stared at the dune ahead, one last pile of sand between her and the peace of the ocean. God, she was so done with feeling sorry for herself, for feeling beat down and pathetic.

The whole point of coming here was to get a fresh start.

She'd had so many opportunities in her lifetime, and she'd squandered them, allowed herself to be shoved into a corner and put up on a shelf.

Well, no more.

No. More.

Derek touched her cheek.

Jumping, Pepper's eyes went to his.

"You don't seem happy now," he murmured.

This man saw way too much.

"You're wrong." She stepped back, crossed the road, and began climbing the path that led over the dune. "I *am* happy. In fact, I'm so content that—"

"You're working as a human directional specialist?" he called.

That threw her for a moment. She glanced back and saw a smile tugging the edges of Derek's mouth up. It blinded her temporarily, like the sun reflecting off a cell phone's screen.

Annoyed, she forced her gaze to the ocean. Stupid, pushy, arrogant, *sexy*—

"A human directional specialist," he repeated as he closed the space between them. "I saw it on a show once. This guy had a sign and called himself a . . . never mind. What's going on? Why are you in Stoneybrook? Is this about the Ferrari?"

She stifled a groan. "You know about the Ferrari?"

He raised a brow, and Pepper mentally smacked herself.

*Of course* he knew about the Ferrari.

Destroy one film set with a really expensive car and everyone was a critic.

She bent and slid off her sandals, reveling for a second in the feel of the warm grains of sand sliding between her toes before taking off in the direction of her cottage.

"It *was* pretty sensational," Derek said and if he sounded amused, it wasn't as if she could begrudge him. More than one gossip show and blog had gotten fodder out of the incident.

"Yes."

Millions of dollars in damaged equipment. One totaled luxury vehicle.

This was why she didn't have nice things.

"Three cameras and an entire set in one fell swoop." He tilted his head, dimples out in full force. "That was pretty impressive, even for you Pep, *er*, Pepper."

"True."

Thankfully, no one had been hurt, which was the sole detail from the incident that she'd been able to take solace in.

She'd gone to set early to prepare for her scene, for the first job she'd actually had to audition for. The director had been one of Hollywood royalty—flush enough to not be swayed by her father's influence.

Her car had been in the shop, recovering from an episode with her mailbox—

But never mind that.

Since her father's driver hadn't been around, she'd thought to handle things herself. She only had to borrow one of the family cars.

How hard could it be, after all, to drive to a new part of Los Angeles?

*Very* hard, apparently. Especially if a woman happened to be taken in by shiny red paint and sleek lines, but was unfamiliar with a stick shift.

She really should have taken a Lyft.

When she didn't say anything further, Derek sighed and continued to walk beside her. "So I'm guessing this isn't about the Ferrari, is it?"

"And they say lawyers aren't smart," she said, tapping her nose.

"Who says that?" he asked, brows drawn down.

"No one."

She was talking nonsense, warring with herself over her urge to draw out the connection with the first boy she'd crushed on, and her need to end the conversation.

Because *of course* her move wasn't about a car. It was about making a name for herself, dammit. Which was something that Derek should understand, considering last she'd heard he'd bucked his family's conventions—legal advice for the rich and famous—and struck out into business on his own—documentary films production.

"Oh, honey, what did you get yourself into *now?*"

Even if she had managed to ignore the condescending use of *honey*, Pepper's temper still would have flared at his arrogance.

"I didn't *get into* anything. I'm trying to find a job." She spun around and poked a finger into his chest. "How is *that* wrong? You're the one who came barreling in, sticking his nose where it doesn't belong."

Pale blue eyes sparked with frustration. "I saved your life," he said, his tone hot. "Usually that garners a thank you, not a dressing down."

Unfortunately, he wasn't completely wrong.

"Thank you," she said.

But he wasn't completely right, either.

"Now butt the hell out of my life and worry about your own."

She turned and walked away.

Or tried to.

"*Oof.*" Pepper hadn't been paying attention to the ocean . . . or its waves, which, *sigh*, she should have known better.

In less than a second, she was on her butt, cold water crashing over her. She pushed her hands against the wet sand and came up sputtering.

The masculine hand on her arm made her life. So. Much. Better.

Derek helped her to her feet and guided her a few feet up shore. She was soaked through, dripping wet and squelching with each step.

"You're right," he said, once they were a safe distance from errant waves. "I shouldn't have pushed. It's just— You're *Paul's* sister."

As if she needed the reminder.

"Thank you." And, unsure if she was thanking him for saving her again or for the pseudo-apology, Pepper slipped free of his grip. Keeping a careful eye on the ocean, she strode away.

Away from cars and men and waves that stole dramatic exits.

She left *everything* on that section of beach.

# FOUR

# WHEN SAND GETS IN REALLY UNCOMFORTABLE PLACES

Derek

DEREK WATCHED Pepper stride up the beach, her clothes clinging to her body like a second skin.

But damn, what a second skin it was—

He deliberately turned away and walked back along the beach.

Pepper really had picked a prime location to relocate to.

Crashing waves, fine sand, quiet town. It wasn't the crystal blue waters and bright, white stretches of the Caribbean—colder water, and a stronger surf here—but it was pretty damn close to heaven.

And he had the feeling that Pepper could use a little more heaven in her life.

He stopped when he reached the path leading to downtown and sank onto the sand. The rough particles were already in his socks, his shoes, streaked up his ankles, so what did it matter? Hell, he could even feel it between his teeth, gritty crystals that crunched as he swallowed.

So he dropped down, toed off his shoes, peeled off his socks, and pondered the enigma that was Pepper.

What were the chances that he'd run into her after all this time?

Pretty good. Considering that *her* father had all but ordered him to Stoneybrook to scout out locations for the documentary on small town America Derek was producing.

The documentary that Peter O'Brien was funding.

Wind gusted, slapping his wet pant legs against his bare ankles. But that couldn't compare to the mental smack against his brain.

If there was one thing that Derek avoided, it was drama.

He'd had too much of it in his thirty years. Too many celebrities threatening to sue over the quality of hair extensions or a bad boob job—and that didn't even account for the women.

Chuckling to himself over his father's time-honored bad joke, Derek leaned back and stared up at the sky.

Pure cerulean blue. Not a cloud in sight. The sun descending behind him.

The perfect type of late afternoon for the beach. Not scalding hot or miserable. The air was laced with a slight chill that made the sand and its intrinsic heat comforting.

Even though the water was too damned cold for his taste. He grimaced and tried to ignore the stiffness that was settling into his damp jeans.

Pepper O'Brien. Pepper-*freaking*-O'Brien.

Who'd suddenly become a woman.

If woman could be spelled t-r-o-u-b-l-e.

Oh, she was definitely gorgeous. Slender, legs for days, with an ass that he wanted to grab on to with both hands.

And right on that particular karmic cue, his cell rang with a very distinct tone.

Peter O'Brien.

Derek wouldn't put it past the man to have read his inappropriate thoughts from three thousand miles away.

Or, maybe more likely, for Pepper's father to have planted spies around town.

"Hello?" he answered, still staring up at the sky.

"Cashette," Peter growled. "What's this about my daughter?"

For a second, Derek was tongue-tied. *Had* Peter somehow known what he was thinking—?

No. That was ridiculous. He hadn't stumbled into one of O'Brien Films' high budget sci-fi flicks. Peter was referring to the car that had nearly plowed his daughter over.

Of course he was.

Which meant that either someone from the crowd had posted something to social media or that Peter really did have spies in town.

All of this crossed Derek's mind in the span of a second because Peter O'Brien wasn't the type of man who was kept waiting for an answer.

Everyone danced to his tune. If he said jump, people jumped. If—well, basically all of the clichés were true.

And so Derek shoved all inappropriate thoughts from his mind and related what had happened. If he somehow underestimated his involvement in Pepper's rescue then it was because he didn't want the man who was, for all intents and purposes, his boss to think he was trying to weasel his way onto his good side.

Or that he'd been on top—and had enjoyed every inch of her body pressed against his—of the man's daughter.

Her hips cradling his, her hair like silk on his fingertips. He'd had the insane urge to kiss the freckles dotting her nose as she'd stared up at him, green eyes wide in stunned surprise.

"My people say you saved her."

The words knocked Pepper's image right from Derek's mind.

A slight shake of his head. "It was nothing."

Peter chuckled. "I think we might have to spring for those permits, after all."

Derek felt a blip of joy—he couldn't afford the filming permits on his current budget. But then reality struck. Because he knew what was coming even before Peter tacked on the next sentence.

"Granted that Pepper stays safely out of trouble."

And *this* is why he didn't normally do business with family . . . or old friends who might as well be family anyway.

There were always strings.

Unfortunately, if he wanted to have this movie made—the one that basically all his contacts had refused to take a chance on—then he'd have to eat crow.

"I'll look out for her, Peter."

"See that you do. My little girl needs someone to keep her in line."

The blip of annoyance surprised Derek. It wasn't Pepper's fault that the woman had driven onto the sidewalk.

"She's doing well," he said. "Trying to get a job and find what she loves."

Derek couldn't fault her that, not when he was trying to do the same thing himself.

"Loves." Peter snorted. "Pepper doesn't know a thing about an honest day's work."

Derek figured that could be true. Pepper had been born not with the proverbial silver spoon, but perhaps a diamond one. Except . . . she'd been out on the sidewalk, sweating in the hot sun without complaint, getting paid what couldn't have been more than minimum wage.

That had to say something about her work ethic.

Life was funny. Odd, funny. Not ha-ha, funny.

For as long as he'd know the O'Briens, he'd seen Pepper exactly as Peter was describing.

A sweet little puppy that trailed along happily, excited to receive a scratch occasionally or some tiny amount of praise. She was the doll on the shelf, something to take down and play with when they were bored, only to be set aside when anything more important came along.

And lots of important things had come along.

Why was Derek just now realizing how truly shitty that was?

He'd discounted Pepper right alongside the rest of them.

Only now, things had changed.

Perhaps, it was the slice of vulnerability in her eyes, the loneliness in her expression, the way her shoulders had fallen just the tiniest bit before she'd determinedly straightened them again.

She needed rescuing.

Alarm bells blared to life in his mind. His inner hero dusted off his super suit, straightened his mask.

Derek's cell clicked in his ear, and he lifted it to glance at the screen, never more relieved to see his mother calling him.

"My other line is ringing," he told Peter. "I'll keep an eye out for Pepper."

"See that you do. I'm trusting you to make sure my little girl stays safe."

Dread settled heavily into his stomach as he hung up.

This project had just gotten a hell of a lot more complicated.

# FIVE

# WINE. IT'S REALLY THE MOST IMPORTANT THING

Pepper

PEPPER STOOD IN HER KITCHEN, eyes locked on the gorgeous view outside the window above her sink. She was trying very hard to find her inner Zen—or at least appear as though she had—because in actuality, she was locked in a crocodile-death-match of a struggle with a bottle of wine and her corkscrew.

Or more aptly, she was trying to open the bottle without impaling herself.

Not the easiest feat for a woman of her abilities, and the danger factor shot up by about a thousand degrees when her phone rang.

The strains of the Imperial March filled the room with the ominous *duh-duh-duh-duhduhduh-duhduhduh* and she half-expected Darth Vader to turn the corner and stride into her kitchen.

Or maybe her imagination was running wild because the person she least wanted to talk to was calling. He was also the person she had no chance of ignoring. Because if she didn't answer the damned phone when her father called, he'd send someone to check on her.

And that didn't exactly gel with her plan to be left the hell alone.

"Hi, Dad," she said, after sliding her finger across the screen to answer the call. She tapped the speakerphone button just in time to hear her father's booming condemnation.

"Pepper O'Brien," he said. "What have you done now?"

*Done?* She picked up the corkscrew from where she'd placed it on the counter to answer his highness's call and jabbed it at the cork.

"I didn't *do* anything."

"That's not what I hear. Bert called and told me you'd almost been run over. What were you doing, trying to get a job like a common person, anyway? We didn't send you to school to—"

"I was just standing on a street corner for Christ's sake!"

The corkscrew slipped, and she bit back a curse as it stabbed her thumb. After setting the bottle and opener down, she grabbed a towel and wrapped it around her finger.

Ouch. That really hurt.

Her father sighed. The same disappointed flow of air she'd heard time and again over the last twenty-four years. It shouldn't affect her. Not after hearing it so often.

Except . . . it did.

"Tone, darling," he admonished. "You know your mother and I raised you better than that, despite the mockery you've made of our family name."

"Your opinion is noted," she muttered, unable to apologize. Not again. Not any longer.

There was a beat of quiet, as though she'd surprised her father with her answer. And since silence wasn't common when Peter O'Brien was around, at least not when he'd gotten started on listing all of her shortcomings, Pepper pressed her advantage. "Did you need something?"

"I—"

"—was checking on me," she interrupted with an innocent voice. "That's very sweet of you. I'm fine but really tired, so I'm going to go to bed. Bye, Dad."

Her father sputtered out a goodbye that she hardly heard because she was already hanging up the phone.

*That went surprisingly well,* she thought with a grin. One that quickly fell away when she noticed the blood seeping through the corner of the towel that was wrapped around her thumb.

"Shit," she muttered, averting her eyes and breathing through her mouth when the dizziness hit her hard.

Propping herself against the countertop, she used it to keep her upright as she half-shuffled, half-walked to the bathroom and pulled out her first aid kit. Considering the amount of mishaps she'd had in her life, she really should be used to blood.

But since that wasn't the case, Pepper stood over the sink and peeled back the towel.

Her mind blurred, screaming a mental, *Gaaaaah!* But she forced her voice to be steady as she talked herself through.

"It's not so bad," she said, staring at her reflection in the mirror until it became clear and focused again. "Just a little cut." Still not looking, she turned on the water and ran her thumb under it, wincing at the feel of the cold water against her injured skin.

It took more than a few minutes of fumbling, made all the harder because she couldn't look at the small wound without her stomach turning, to get it clean, dry, and wrapped in a bandage. But she did it and managed to walk back into the kitchen with a little *pep* in her step as she approached the wine bottle.

Corkscrew. Check. Laptop open. Check. YouTube video for Easiest Way to Open a Bottle of Wine cued up. Check. Said bottle of wine. Check.

She could do this.

Place sharp point on cork. Turn. Turn. Turn—

And sigh.

She'd split the cork.

"Dammit," she muttered. Next time, she was buying a box of wine. She didn't even care. At least *that* had a spout. Or hell, maybe she'd get a Camelbak and fill it with Chardonnay, or one of those wine purse things with the nozzle on one end. She glanced down at the cork, now seemingly out of reach of the corkscrew, and sucked her bottom lip between her teeth. Then she snatched a steak knife from the drawer, ready to do that cutting-off-the-top-of-the-bottle thing she'd seen fancy chefs do.

Wine. It needed to be happening now.

Except. She stopped. Because *knives?* Really? Who was she kidding?

After putting the instrument of death—at least in her hands —back into the drawer, Pepper glanced around the kitchen and chose the object least likely to harm her.

A wooden spoon.

Turning it over, she stuck the handle in the opening and shoved the cork down into the bottle.

Victory was hers!

Then she reached into the drawer and pulled out her longest twisty-twirly straw. Because know what? She wasn't really living life if she couldn't drink wine through a twisty-twirly straw every once in a while.

"See?" she said to herself, grabbing her wine and heading out onto her deck. "You might not get things done the way everyone expects but you can still do things your own way."

She sank into a chair and stared out at the waves, the evening's darkness seeping into the horizon like ink into paper.

Peace. This was a place she could find peace.

Lips to the straw, she sucked up a large sip of Chardonnay.

And promptly choked on a fragment of cork.

Oh, yeah. This was *her* life.

Peace was fleeting, and it really sucked sometimes.

# SIX

# WHO NEEDS BEAUTY SLEEP?

PEPPER *WANTED* to be one of those people who loved getting up early in the morning, but the fact was she loved sleep.

Her bed was the best.

Soft blankets, cuddly pillows, a cozy mattress. Add in a window, cracked open an inch to let in the soothing sounds of waves, and she rarely wanted to move before the sun was high in the sky.

Unfortunately, her friend, and neighbor, had a different idea.

The doorbell rang.

With a groan, Pepper rolled over, covered her head with one of her perfect, cuddly, *comfortable* pillows, and ignored the chime.

Rylie would go away.

Pepper realized that she'd severely underestimated the tenacity of her friend when her voice echoed through the slightly open window.

"Ms. Pepper!"

Except, since Rylie was only six, it sounded more like "Ms. Pepah!"

She sat up and met bright brown eyes through the glass.

"Come play!"

An unwilling smile curved her lips. Once Rylie had realized that Pepper was alone in town—or friendless as the little monster called it—the six year-old had decided it was her duty to make sure Pepper was never lonely.

Even when she wanted to sleep in.

"I'm tired," she muttered.

She winced at the sunlight pouring into the room. Okay fine, it wasn't so much that she was tired as the entire bottle of wine she consumed the previous night.

Turned out twisty straws could be dangerous when it came to wine drinking.

"You promised we'd build a sandcastle!"

"Rylie, where are—" Shannon, Rylie's mother, appeared breathless outside the window. "Oh no! I'm sorry, Pepper. I told her to leave you alone."

"We're going to build a sandcastle," Rylie said, her bottom lip jutting out.

"You need to wait until Ms. Pepper is available, not just barge over here." She plunked her hands onto her hips. "You're only six years old. You can't wander around without an adult."

That lip protruded farther. "You said I was a big girl."

"You are," Shannon said. "Which is why you need to understand big kid rules. And one of those is not running off."

Rylie looked so sad that Pepper wanted to say it was okay, to go out and build a hundred castles with the little girl. But Shannon was right. The world could be dangerous and if Rylie got too close to the ocean, misjudged a wave . . . Pepper shuddered to think of it.

"I need to do a few things first," she told Rylie, pushing from the bed and padding over to the window. She raised it and continued the conversation drive-through-style. "If you give me a couple of hours, I can meet you for lunch on the beach."

"Really?"

Pepper shoved back a strand of hair. "So long as your mom says it's okay."

Shannon smiled gratefully. "That's okay with me. I'll make up a picnic basket."

"Oh," Pepper said. "You don't have to do that. I can—"

"No!" Shannon and Rylie responded in unison.

A girl makes gritty peanut butter and jelly sandwiches *one* time. She made a face. "I'll have you know that sand is just a little extra fiber."

Shannon ruffled Rylie's hair. "This one ate enough sand as a baby to make her own beach. I'll pass on the extra fiber."

They waved, calling out a goodbye as they turned and walked toward their own bungalow.

"Bring your shoveling arms, Pepper!"

She flexed. "They're already attached."

The sound of youthful giggles followed her into the bathroom.

A shower rinsed away the last of Pepper's wine brain, and she slipped on her flip flops, a T-shirt, and a ratty pair of shorts. Experience told her that sand was going to go everywhere—and she meant *everywhere*.

Rylie was a . . . vigorous digger.

She prattled about her kitchen for a few minutes, burning a piece of toast and starting to scrape off the blackened bits before tossing the whole thing in the trash.

What was the point?

Whatever Shannon packed for lunch was bound to be much more delicious.

It didn't take much for Pepper to locate the duo once she'd

walked out onto her front porch. Rylie's cheerful voice carried over the dunes, ear-piercing and smile-inducing all at once.

She waved and took the stairs two at a time.

Unfortunately, not because she meant to.

Her foot missed that first step, and she ended up kind of lurch-walking down the other two, grabbing at the handle to prevent a head-first landing in the sand.

"You're funny, Ms. Pepper," Rylie said, having run over while she did her impersonation of a klutzy crab.

"Well, you're funny *looking*."

Rylie gave her a look that was way older than her six years and held out a shovel. "That's not funny. Now come on. I want this one to be big!"

Considering that Pepper had spent near on three hours shoveling and compacting sand the last time, she shuddered to think of what *big* would mean.

Nevertheless, she followed Rylie's skipping form down the beach, the picnic basket and three chairs set out around a brightly striped blanket. Shannon was curled up in one, a book in her lap.

"How soon until Brian is home?" Pepper asked.

Brian was Shannon's husband, who travelled frequently for his work as an airline consultant.

"Tuesday." Her friend sighed. "Four more days."

"And when does school start back up?"

"Wednesday." Another sigh. "I'd hoped to take a family vacation this summer." Her lips twisted into a rueful smile. "Guess that's not happening."

Shannon taught third grade at the local elementary school. Not because they needed the money, but because Brian was never home. Pepper didn't like the man for that reason—she herself was the product of a father who'd worked too much—but she especially didn't like the lonely look in Shannon's eyes.

If Brian wasn't careful, he'd lose touch with both wife and daughter.

"We need more wet sand," Pepper told Rylie, who was nearly wriggling out of her swimsuit in excitement. "Can you grab some water?"

Rylie rolled her eyes. "That's code for girl talk." But she grabbed a bucket and headed for the ocean.

"She's six going on forty," she murmured.

Shannon sighed. "I know."

She set down the shovel, spun on the blanket and faced her friend. "Are you okay?"

Shannon's eyes were on her daughter as she skipped along the wave line. "That girl has too much personality. Way too much."

"She'll keep you on your toes, that's for sure," Pepper said and waited. Shannon needed to talk or she wouldn't have made the vacation comment. And if there was one thing Pepper was good at, it was listening.

Mainly because it involved zero amount of bodily coordination.

Finally, Shannon sighed, hands smacking against her thighs. "Brian has been home four days this last month. Four days!"

Shit. She hadn't realized it was that bad. "Four out of thirty isn't much."

"No, it's not, and when I asked if he could cut back his traveling he said, flat out, no! He's missing everything, her first lost tooth, the first time she rode her bike without training wheels." Shannon gripped her book, mangling the edges. "Hell, he wouldn't have even made it for her first day of school on Wednesday if I hadn't thrown the epic hissy fit to end all hissy fits. Then he acted like coming back two days early from his trip was a grand inconvenience."

She broke off, chest heaving, tanned skin flushed red, blue eyes full of hurt.

And that hurt Pepper.

"What did you do when your dad was away for months at a time on set?" Shannon asked and Pepper startled. Shannon had never mentioned Pepper's dad before. They hadn't been friends that long, only since the beginning of summer when she'd moved in and mostly because Rylie was a force to be reckoned with, dragging Pepper along until she and her mom had become almost involuntary friends, bound over their shared amusement for a six-year-old.

But though their start might not have been traditional, Pepper and Shannon had a lot in common, and she genuinely enjoyed spending time with the other woman.

Of course, by some unspoken rule, they'd never mentioned anything more than what was superficially obvious. A shared love of wine, not being able to resist a little girl's charm, bad reality TV.

They'd had plenty to talk about.

It had just never been anything particularly meaningful.

Until that moment.

"My dad was gone more than he was home," Pepper agreed. "I guess I just learned to live without him."

Learned to stop trying so hard to please him when he did finally make it home.

"That's what I'm afraid of. I don't want her to have to live—"

Pepper spun around at Shannon's cut off sentence. Had Rylie—

"Holy. Shit," Shannon murmured.

"Language," Pepper teased, breathing a sigh as she spied Rylie safe and sound. The little girl stood near the water's edge, shouting at a man over the waves. "You're supposed to be getting ready for the school year."

"Shh." Shannon swatted at Pepper's shoulder. "Someone sees a specimen of manhood like *that* and language doesn't matter."

"I can't believe that you just said *specimen of manhood.* Gross."

"Shut up. He's hot."

"He's something all right," she muttered, her breath catching despite herself.

Because the man, who was walking out of the waves as though he was Jason Momoa in *Aquaman,* was Derek.

Shannon practically moaned.

"Jesus, girl. Get it together," Pepper groused. "Of course he's not wearing a shirt."

"Thank God for that," Shannon breathed.

Pepper couldn't be mad at her, not really. Not when water sluiced down Derek's tanned chest, all glisteny and shit. He sparkled like Edward Cullen, except ripped and without of risk of the midday sun.

"He still has a freaking six-pack." Pepper tilted her head toward the sky, mentally cursed whatever God was at work up there. "Really?"

"Yes, he does. Wait—" Shannon tore her eyes away. "What do you mean *still?*"

"It doesn't matter."

"Like hell it doesn't." Shannon dropped her voice even though Derek, who'd completed his god-like-rising-from-the-waves business and had paused next to Rylie as she continued chatting his ear off. "You *know* Mr. Ass-So-Tight-I-Could-Bounce-A-Dime?"

"You haven't even seen his ass!" Pepper protested.

Shannon lifted one brown eyebrow. "Do I need to?"

A sigh as she flopped onto her back on the blanket and threw an arm over her eyes. "No." Derek's ass was definitely grade A. "It could probably bounce a quarter."

When there was no reply, Pepper lifted her arm and peered out.

Caribbean blue eyes stared back at her.

"What does bounce a quarter mean, Mommy?" Rylie asked.

Derek smiled.

# SEVEN

# WHEN YOUR BODY IS AN A-HOLE

"REALLY?" Pepper mouthed to Shannon, who shrugged, lips twitching, the jerk.

"Hey, Pepper," Derek said.

She tried valiantly to save herself. "And that's why Hemsworth is my favorite celebrity Chris. His as—"

Shannon cleared her throat.

"Language!" Rylie chimed.

The world was conspiring against her.

"How about that sand castle?" she said, picking back up a bucket and shovel and, most importantly, ignoring Derek as she strode by him.

Five feet away, at the perfect stretch of beach—just wet enough to form turrets without getting stuck in the buckets—she dropped to her knees, bent, and started digging.

"Speaking of asses." Derek's voice was low and wicked and sent every nerve cell in her body zinging.

She ignored the little zip down her spine, kept shoveling sand into her bucket.

He plunked down next to her and held the green plastic container steady. "Come on, it was funny."

Another scoop of sand and it was nearly full.

"Should we talk about nonsense then?" he asked. "Like is Hemsworth really your favorite Chris?"

"It's actually a tossup between him and Evans."

He choked.

Hopefully on sand as she all but tossed the last shovelful into the bucket.

Though it was probably on laughter.

She patted the sand down and turned the bucket over.

"That's—" Derek froze as he looked down at the turret, perfect peaks surrounding its top, the sides smooth and sleek.

Girl could build a sandcastle.

And by girl, she meant her.

Rolling her eyes at herself, she began filling the bucket again.

"I've never seen anyone able to make it turn out so perfect, not on a bucket that size."

Were they really discussing sand pail size?

"Turns out there actually *is* something I'm good at," she muttered. "As hard as that is to believe."

"That's not what I meant."

"I know it's just sand—"

"Pepper."

"But occasionally—"

"*Pepper.*"

"I—"

Warm fingers encircled her wrist, halting her angry shoveling. His other hand cupped her chin and tilted her head up. She wanted to look away, to not be snared in his gaze. It was dangerous, looking at him, studying him, *wanting* him. She couldn't fall into his trap.

And Derek Cashette was definitely a trap—albeit one wrapped up as a gorgeous specimen of manhood.

Her lips twitched.

Blue eyes darkened to navy, a calloused thumb slid up her jaw to trace the little curve that had appeared. "What is it?"

She found herself leaning in, his voice sending a shiver down her spine. It was laced with heat, that old Derek charm coming into play, and *that* was enough to have her pulling back, turning her gaze to the ocean instead of him.

"We need four more towers!" Rylie shouted, skidding to a halt two inches behind the first turret. "And a moat! And—"

She was off and running. Saving Pepper from making a fool of herself.

Or more of one, anyway.

---

SAND ON HER BARE TOES.

The little flecks rubbed against the soles of her feet, caked over her nails. Warm on top, cool beneath.

And if there was ever a metaphor for her life.

Pepper felt cold inside. Empty. Unfulfilled and anxious.

She wished she could say that this was a new feeling, but it had always been that way—the gnawing, clawing need to prove herself. The desire to live up to the family name, wanting to stand out, to be spectacular . . . when she was really just normal.

*Normal.*

Why did it always feel like an insult?

A wave slid up the shore, swept over her feet, rinsing the sand from her toes, hitching behind her ankles and tugging her toward the dark abyss.

Moonlight sucked the color from the sand and water, transforming her backyard into an old black and white movie. It felt spooky, those shades of gray and ivory, like the set of a horror flick or, perhaps, another world. Though if she turned her head, reality intruded. Houses lined the beach, their windows gleaming like bright yellow lights, illuminating sand pails and chairs, porches and bikes strewn haphazardly in side yards.

So Pepper kept her gaze pointedly on the shoreline.

Reality, no thanks. Not right now.

Her ankle and back were stiff from the near miss during her stint at human directional advertising—and no, her lips didn't twitch at the reminder of Derek—not to mention all of the sand castle building. But she hadn't been lying when she'd told Derek at the time that she'd had worse.

A broken wrist, two black eyes, one torn ligament in her foot, bruised ribs . . . and that was just in the last year—

Not really, it was more like the last five, but that was her brother's go-to joke.

Clearly, her family wasn't famous for being comedians.

But none of this reminiscing and wishing things were different was helping her decide what she needed to do, how she could change her life into something worthwhile. She couldn't write a book . . . well, she *could,* but then her father would never talk to her again. Although— Pepper tapped her chin—that might not be a bad thing.

No. Ix-nay on the tell-all book exposing Hollywood for exactly what most people thought it was—vapid, plastic, back-stabbing, and filled with only the occasional nice person.

Reality TV?

Oh, plenty of those offers had come in. But hell if she was going to give people another way to make fun of her.

Jobless, klutzy Pepper O'Brien.

Yeah. No thanks.

And regular jobs weren't likely to work out—her previous exploits with the granny mobile riding the sidewalk like a cowboy clinging to a bull telling her that much.

Perhaps she could nanny?

But who would trust *her* with their kids?

So, circling back to why she was here. Stuck. Everything was fine, she was safe, had money to keep her going, but nothing made her feel excited inside. Wasn't she supposed to be jumping out of bed in the morning, eager to get to work? Her father and brother certainly were.

But then again, they had something to be eager for.

While she . . . she had nothing.

Sighing, Pepper took a few steps back, plopped to the sand, and—

"Shit!" Shifting, she reached behind her and extracted a stick. Though she supposed the technical term was driftwood. "Really?" she exclaimed, glaring at the offending piece of lumber.

She curled her fingers around the wood and pulled her hand back, ready to chuck it into the ocean but something stopped it.

Maybe it was the texture. Smooth, even though it looked rough.

Maybe it was the weight. So much lighter than she expected.

Maybe it was the moonlight highlighting all the ups and downs and curves of that little stick.

But for whatever reason, Pepper palmed the piece of driftwood and slid it into her pocket.

And when she got home, she found that it looked just perfect perched on the windowsill above her sink.

There was something about the way that wood looked . . .

# EIGHT
## NOBODY LIKES A WEDDING

Derek

DEREK TOOK a picture of the wooden sign proclaiming Stoneybrook and mentally compared it to the other towns he'd visited in the last months. This one was vibrant, the contrasting blue and white paint bright and fresh. The others had been missing letters or had peeling paint, most were faded and some were falling down.

Stoneybrook was lucky.

Nowadays, small-town America was a tough place to make a life.

But here, kids raced up and down the sidewalk, enjoying one last summer weekend before school started. Ice cream cones, sandy toes, blooming flowers. His mind categorized each shot, almost as quickly as the shutter on his camera flickered open and closed.

He'd contrast this town and another he'd visited.

Bram, Missouri had boomed when a paper mill opened on the river running through the city then had almost collapsed when that mill eventually closed. But Bram was now going through a revival, and with a little luck and some permit fees from his film, it might just be able to complete that comeback.

Derek made a mental checkmark on his to-do list and was tucking his camera away when his cell phone rang.

He sighed and lifted it to his ear, seeing it was Paul, his old friend and Pepper's brother. Never let it be said that the O'Briens weren't on it with their P names. Even Pepper's mom was named Poppy, though that was a nickname since her legal name was actually Matilda. Where Poppy had come from, Derek had no clue.

Peter had probably demanded his wife find a suitable P substitute.

In Derek's experience, Peter was good at being demanding, and most especially good at being demanding with women.

He winced, knowing that uncharitable thoughts about his investor didn't bode well for the project.

"Hello?"

Shit. Derek shook himself, realizing he'd answered the phone without actually saying anything. "Paul! Hey man, what's up?"

"I'm getting married."

"That's great." It wasn't, really, because the woman Paul was with was a former friend of Pepper's . . . who was also kind of a bitch. Still, Derek knew if Paul was happy, then he could tolerate Summer—

Although, she would probably soon be known as Petunia or something equally horrific that kept up that time-honored O'Brien tradition of P names. Paul kept talking over Derek's inner monologue, prattling on about production schedules and having to hurry things around before—

"Next month?" Derek broke in when he realized what Paul was saying. "You're getting *married* next month?"

"She's not pregnant," Paul said. "It's the schedule. O'Brien Films has four projects about to go, and I need to be there."

To be fair, with such a rush job on the wedding, Derek would have probably thought that Summer *was* pregnant. Still, hurrying what was supposed to be one of the most important moments of someone's life so that Paul could get back to work left a bad taste in Derek's mouth.

Since he didn't think that would go over well, Derek just said, "You tell me when, and I'll be there."

"Thanks, man," Paul said and paused, a note of remorse in his tone. "I don't want you to think that we're not—well, I asked Andy to be my best man. I was hoping you'd be a groomsman."

"Of course. I'd be honored—" Not exactly. But, more importantly, it was pretty much the only thing to be said when asked to be in a wedding. "There are perks to just being a groomsman. No speech."

Paul gave a laugh, and it was forced.

Derek got it. They'd been tight in high school and college, but lives changed and since he'd quit the law firm, his interactions with old friends just weren't the same. He couldn't quite enjoy the Hollywood scene as much, not when so much of it was complete and utter bullshit.

People grew apart, pulled back. He and Paul were no different, and Derek thought it was probably for the best. The person he'd been in the past wasn't something he was proud of.

But those old ties didn't necessarily dissolve just because he'd changed.

And now . . . he was a groomsman in Paul's wedding, and making a film with Paul and Pepper's father.

Ties strengthening.

He ignored the blip of alarm that came from that thought.

"So, no hard feelings?" Paul asked.

"Are you kidding?" Derek said, forcing himself to focus on

the conversation, on doing and saying the right thing. This was Paul's wedding, not time for him to have a crisis of conscience. "I'm happy for you, regardless of my bridal party position. Feel free to demote me to usher or flower girl as need be."

Paul snorted. "That would be a sight." A beat. "But seriously, thanks, man. Andy thought with Pepper being the maid of honor that things would be easier—"

"Pepper's the maid of honor?"

"Of course, she is. She and Summer are super close, and Dad—" Paul stopped. "Anyway, with such a short lead time, Pepper made sense. Especially since we're using the date and time that she'd originally booked for her wedding."

"*What?*"

"It made sense," Paul said, rightly a touch defensive. And this is where he lost Derek because a rushed marriage was an idiotic idea. A rushed marriage taking place at the same place and time of his sister's cancelled wedding was even more so. "Dad couldn't get the deposit back, and Pepper had already made all the arrangements."

Paul was using Pepper's discarded wedding for his own.

What the fuck?

Next Paul would be telling him he'd recycled Pepper's engagement ring because she didn't need it any longer.

Anger sat like a heavy ball in Derek's gut.

He was starting to understand why she looked so sad.

"Paul," he began. "You know, I don't think—"

"I'll email you the details," Paul told him before saying goodbye and hanging up.

Derek stood for a moment on the sidewalk, people murmuring soft "Excuse me's" as they moved past him, but he hardly noticed. His emotions were tangled and confused.

Pepper had always been a conundrum.

*No.* She'd been a joke.

It was *his* internal shift that was the confusing part.

Maybe Derek was experiencing a mid-life crisis. Yeah, sure. He was almost thirty and going completely deranged.

Or maybe . . . he'd just never given Pepper enough credit.

Which was perhaps the reason he pocketed his phone and instead of heading to the bed and breakfast he was staying at, Derek turned in the direction of the beach.

It took less than ten minutes to reach Pepper's cottage.

And he knew it was *her* cottage because she was sitting on the back porch, still in her pajamas—a tiny pair of flannel shorts and a tank top that was almost illegally tight.

Derek forced his eyes up from the exposed skin of her thighs, and his gaze caught on a pair of breasts that—

He swallowed, palms itching with the sudden need to touch.

He wrenched his focus higher still. To the smooth skin of her throat, the soft plumpness of her lips, the . . . hurt in her eyes.

"Hey," he said, Lothario in action.

"Hi," she said and promptly burst into tears.

Not to be an asshole, and knowing full well that he sounded like one anyway, but . . . women had never been confusing to Derek. He'd understood their needs, their triggers, how to charm his way into their pants. Of course, that was when charming into many different pairs of pants was still exciting. At this point in his life, he'd gone nearly a year without sleeping with a woman. And of course, Pepper wasn't just a woman.

She was . . . different.

And perhaps that wasn't the bad thing everyone always made it seem.

She was herself. Not plastic. Not fake. Not—

She sniffed and turned away, hands lifting and covering her face.

Derek had frozen at her tears—instead of moving in to console her as he would have done any other woman—and in the time it took for him to get his feet moving, she had stifled her sobs and was rubbing an arm across her eyes.

"Excuse me," she said, pushing up from her chair and turning for the house. "My allergies are acting up."

Derek sat down, parking himself in a comfy wicker Adirondack that was one of four surrounding a white woven table. Bright blue cushions dotted each seat and back. Pepper's deck was homey and cozy and definitely not the ornate lines and heavy finishes that were typical of an O'Brien. Gold leaf, intricate scrollwork, and dark mahogany wood would be more at home in an O'Brien house.

Then again, Peter and Poppy O'Brien didn't exactly do sand.

It was too messy.

They preferred to live in the hills above, looking gleefully down on their minions, and to just visit the beach.

Less sand in the private jet's carpets that way.

"Your allergies make you burst into sudden tears?" he asked when she sniffed again.

"At the sight of you?" She spun back to face him and leveled a glare in his direction. "Yes. Sudden and unexplained tears are common."

A drop of moisture hung on the edge of her lashes.

Derek wanted to reach forward to brush it away.

Stupid.

Pepper turned for the house again, leaving him sitting on the deck feeling incredibly unsure of himself.

"Well?"

She was in the doorway, still glaring, still beautiful as hell.

He raised a brow.

"Come inside already."

He watched her as she whirled around, her bright red hair fanning out behind her like a cape, drawing his gaze down, down . . . too far down.

Derek swallowed, forced his eyes away from the shorts so barely there they were nearly obscene.

This was a terrible idea.

# NINE

# TEARS ARE GOOD FOR THE SKIN

Pepper

SHE BRUSHED her fingers across the surface of the piece of driftwood she'd found on the beach the night before as she waited to see if Derek would come in. The stick had dried out, turning from almost black to a soft grayish brown. Her mind spun, an image forming in her brain when her eyes drifted to the cup of shells she'd also collected that happened to be sitting next to the wood.

Then sparkle of sunlight drifting through the clear glass of the kitchen window caught her gaze.

The textured creams of the shells.

The gray-brown of the wood.

The crystalline glass.

Hmm.

A soft *click* broke the spell.

"Paul called you?" Derek asked, shutting the door leading out to the deck and moving the few feet through into her kitchen. The cottage was the smallest house she'd ever lived in, but she liked the close quarters a lot better than the endless empty rooms that featured heavily in her family's homes.

"No." She heaved out a silent sigh, leaving the shells and glass and wood for the time being, and rotated to face him. "Summer."

"So you know."

About having to play nice with her jerk of an ex-fiancé? About wondering why she kept putting herself through this instead of finally telling her family to fuck off?

Maybe she was a perpetual optimist.

Or maybe she was . . . pathetic.

"I know about the wedding." *Sigh*. "And I know about Andy."

"And . . . are you okay with it?"

Good God. The last person she wanted to play Dr. Phil with was Derek. He didn't need to know the push-pull that was going on in her head, how she was constantly warring with herself over what to do with her family.

Plus, in most ways she *was* okay with it. She didn't want to get back with Andy. He was a jerk, plain and simple, and *she'd* broken things off with him. It was just that—

It was supposed to be her wedding.

"I'm thrilled for Paul and Summer," she forced herself to say. "I'm glad they're happy."

In *their* way. Which basically meant they were obsessed with the business. They lived to make that next blockbuster. That next hundred million for the company.

"And you're comfortable with being the—"

"Maid of honor?" A tight curve of lips before she crossed to the fridge and pulled out two bottles of water. She and Summer had been close in another time, but their paths had veered as definitively as the proverbial fork in the road.

Pepper really wanted the wine staring at her from the

second shelf, but she'd been drinking too much lately, so instead she closed the door, handed a water bottle to Derek, then cracked her own.

He glanced down at it for a moment, hesitating.

Pepper knew what he was seeing. The thin plastic packaging because the bottle was from one of those bulk packs, found in every grocery store across the country.

Twenty-four bottles for $3.99. Normal.

As opposed to the glass cylinders in her family's fridge. Fifty dollars a pop.

And they were both still tap water.

But O'Briens didn't do normal. They did expensive cars, antique furniture, private jets, and fancy bottled water.

The difference was . . . Pepper had changed.

Which wasn't something she could trace back to a specific event. More, she'd finally come to terms with exactly how ridiculous the lifestyle her parents were pushing was. She'd worn designer clothes, and it hadn't made her happy, hadn't filled the hole inside her. She'd driven expensive cars, and that didn't make the mailboxes any less easy for her to avoid.

Money didn't stop her fiancé from cheating.

Money didn't make her any less of a screw up.

Her throat was tight when Derek spoke again. "Want to talk about it?"

"Talk about what?" The wedding? Andy? The fact that she was twenty-four years old and experiencing a midlife crisis. Her eyes flashed to his, and she saw the exact opposite thing she wanted. Pity.

Derek felt sorry for her.

Cool.

"The wedding," he said.

"Nope."

"Pepper." He put his bottle down, took a step toward her.

"Derek," she countered, gripping her own in front of her like it was a shield.

"It's okay to be upset."

Her eyes stung again, and—no, dammit, she was done with tears over Andy—she let her head flop back, lids closed as she silently waited for the blasted moisture to go away. Maybe she'd get the ducts removed like her mother's friend had. Seemed better than letting the leaky, traitorous bastards rule the roost.

And *that* Hollywood reminder was enough to dry her eyes.

"Pep," he began.

"Don't." Her head popped up—

*Crack.*

"Ow," she muttered, rubbing her forehead when it had clonked into Derek's nose.

And cue blood.

Her knees went wobbly and she wavered.

*This* was her life.

Derek muttered a curse as he reached past her and grabbed a towel, pressing it to his nose. His *bleeding* nose.

Just the thought made her mind swim.

"Sit," he ordered, pushing her down into a chair at the kitchen table and turning for the sink.

"I'm—"

"*Sit.*"

She sat.

"Close your eyes."

The sound of running water echoed through the room, and then Pepper felt a cool cloth land on the back of her neck. She startled, nearly lurching out of the chair.

"Relax," Derek murmured, wiping the cotton across her forehead. It felt fabulous, that gentle cold, and her dizziness began to fade.

She carefully slit open her eyes and glanced up at him, and

though he still had the towel pressed to his nose, and there was a drop or two of blood on the pale blue material, Pepper hardly registered it.

Because Derek was mere inches away.

He had a scar at the corner of his mouth.

His bottom lip looked like a cushy pillow that hers wanted to rest against.

His eyes were hot—heated pools of navy that swept over her face, assessing.

Shit. She wanted him to kiss her. To drop his mouth to hers and make her forget about the blood, about the wedding, about her ex, about her family . . .

He didn't.

Instead, he whipped around and strode for the sink, wrenching on the water with enough force to rattle her little jar of shells. It wobbled on the shelf . . . and fell, landing in the sink, shattering against the white porcelain.

"Oh shit, Pepper," Derek said. "I'm sor—"

"It's fine," she said, jumping to her feet, keeping her tone deliberately light as she crossed to him. "It's just a jar. Why don't you use the bathroom sink to take care of *that*"—she waved a hand at his face—"while I clean this up? It's the first door on the left."

She pushed her way in front of him and, predictably, he backed up.

*Don't touch Pepper. You might catch her klutziness.*

"I—"

"Go."

Derek went. She sighed and then, blinking away the feeling-sorry-for-herself vibes, began to carefully gather up the pieces of glass.

The sharp edges sparkled in the sunlight, gathering little rainbows.

She picked up the piece of driftwood, placed it amongst the mess, and somehow it made sense.

Carefully, she scooped up the pieces that worked—large chunks of glass, the shells, the hunk of wood—and put them into a bowl that she tucked safely in a corner of the counter.

The rest she tossed in the trash before rinsing out the sink, managing to only slice herself once with a glass sliver.

She was staring out the window, stinging finger in her mouth when she heard Derek's voice.

"Let me see," he murmured.

And then he was there. Close enough that the scent of his aftershave swept over her, that she felt the heat of his body through her clothes.

She dropped her hand. "It's nothing."

He didn't speak, just picked up her wrist, inspecting the hurt finger. After a moment, he bent and lifted her hand to his mouth. His lips brushed the tiny cut, and watching his mouth touch where hers had been only a few seconds before made her insides go all squirmy.

She wanted him.

Then again, she always had.

"Better?" he said and maybe Pepper was imagining things, but was his voice almost . . . husky?

Hallucinate much?

Maybe her Keurig had given her the Mushroom Blend.

She snorted, and Derek's head tilted to the side. "What is it?"

"Nothing." A tug, but he refused to give her hand back.

His free palm came up and cupped her cheek. "I like this smile," he said. "A little smirk, the way your lips curve up." One finger brushed the corner of her mouth. "Just wish it would make it all the way to your eyes. I wish I could make you feel better. Help you—"

Melting. His words made her melt.

Until the last.

She yanked free. "I'm not some charity project," she snapped. "I'm fine, okay? Big deal, I have to play nice with my former fiancé at what was supposed to be *my* wedding. I've pretended plenty of times in my life, and I can do it again. It's not like I want to get back with the cheating asshole."

Screw it. She crossed to the fridge and yanked out the bottle of wine.

Derek plucked it from her fingers. "It's barely noon."

"And you're not my father," she snapped, reaching for the bottle.

He held it aloft. "Drinking won't make it better."

"It'll make me care less." She launched herself at the wine, all but plastering her body against his in the process.

"Andy cheated on you?"

She froze, stepped back. "I didn't say that."

"Actually—"

A sharp shake of her head. "It doesn't matter."

"It matters to *me*." He set the bottle on the table and came to stand in front of her. "Is that why . . ."

She sighed then figured she might as well get this conversation over with. Mostly, because it would reunite her with her wine sooner. But also because if the Derek of now was similar to the Derek she'd known as a teenager then stubbornness wasn't a quality he was lacking in.

"Why I left?" He nodded.

"No," she said. "Leaving was my father's idea." Something she'd grabbed on to. Something she should have had the smarts or strength to think of herself. Get away from the judging eyes, the mean girls, the toxic environment. "He wanted me to let the press blow over after the Christian Incident."

"What's the"—Derek did actual air quotes, which should

have been dorky, but instead was cute . . . *ugh*—"Christian Incident?"

"You really don't know?" He shook his head and she stifled a sigh. *Shit.* Was there seriously a person on the planet who didn't know? Apparently so. So, she just laid it out there. "When I hit Christian Strand in the face with his own Oscar."

"*On purpose?*" he asked, eyes wide.

She really should be better at telling the story at this point. "Of course not."

"Then—"

"Sit down," she said, walking to a drawer and extracting the bottle opener. She handed it to Derek. "I'll tell you, but I'm going to need wine."

# TEN
## WINE IS EVERYTHING

Derek

HE PULLED the cork from the bottle, poured some of the Chardonnay into two glasses, and waited for Pepper to tell him.

She did, but not until after she'd downed a large portion of her glass.

"I'm not a closet alcoholic," she said, seeing him watch her.

"Never said you were."

"Your eyes say enough."

He took a sip of his own wine, enjoyed the notes of cherry, the bitter tang on his tongue, the pleasant warmth in his stomach. "This is good."

A shrug. "I know wine."

Lifting his glass, Derek said, "Case in point."

Pepper sighed. "Do you honestly not know what happened with Christian?"

"I haven't been spending a lot of time in the usual Hollywood circles."

"Why not?" She traced her finger along the top of her glass. "That's where you live."

"*Used* to live," he said. "And things in L.A.—they just get old after a while."

"That they do."

"I wanted something . . ."

Pepper met his eyes. "Different?"

They stared at each other, a perfect moment of understanding passing between them. The connection was one he'd never thought possible. With just a single word, Pepper showed she understood him more than even his own family had.

"Yes," he murmured.

"I've wanted something different my whole life." A self-deprecating smile. "Unfortunately, it's been impossible to find something that fits."

"Hence the human-directional advertising."

She laughed darkly. "No, *that* was more about making some money, because I'm tired of asking my father to pay my way."

Derek considered her . . . and then himself. He'd short-changed Pepper, never thinking of her as anything but an accessory to the family business. He should have given her more credit. Especially, since he'd left *his* family's company in order to make his own way.

"I know," she muttered, sarcasm in every syllable, "it's surprising, right? Wanting to make my own money. Turns out, however, that an art history degree doesn't create a lot of opportunities when trying to make a living."

"And this has to do with Christian how?"

"Obscurely." She closed her eyes for a heartbeat before opening them, the emerald depths heavy with emotion. "I begged Christian for a job because I thought it was a good, happy medium. Pulling in an up-and-coming celebrity who hadn't made an O'Brien Film yet, meeting other new talents. Of course, my father nearly had a stroke when he learned that I was *assisting,* so it wouldn't have lasted much longer anyway. It's just . . ."

Pepper paused. Derek waited.

She shook her head. "It's not a surprise that I'm different. I've always been. You remember the birthday party, right?"

"Yeah."

The infamous Birthday Party. Yes, with capital letters.

It had been Paul's eighteenth, and no way could Derek forget it.

"I wanted to do something nice for him," she said, "so I rented the animal company. He loved snakes, and I thought he would enjoy it."

Paul *had* loved snakes.

Unfortunately, his girlfriend and the bevy of other teenage girls hadn't.

"When that baby boa constrictor slipped out of my hands and landed on Mandy"—who'd run screaming on the wet pool deck and ended up with a broken leg—"it was an accident." She sighed. "But then again they always are."

"That wasn't your fault," he said. "Paul's girlfriend should have known better than to run on water-soaked concrete."

"What's the saying?" Pepper twisted her wine glass in her fingers. "Lightning doesn't strike the same place twice? But it *has* struck. Multiple times. And the only common factor is me." Her voice dropped. "I'm toxic."

"I don't think—"

She cut him off, mask sliding over her face, tone going chipper, fake smile locking into place.

It made him sad.

"So, anyway, Christian's maid was ill, and I thought I'd help her out. His house was a big place, and she was getting older," she added when he lifted a brow. "But then I got a little carried away when I saw the Oscar."

"Carried away how?" he asked.

A sigh. "I . . . Christian surprised me. I was dusting it, and well, he came up close behind me . . . I turned, and when I did . . . I somehow hit him in the face—broke his nose and gave him two black eyes before an important call back."

Oh shit.

"*Then* I dropped the statue." Her eyes drifted to the table. "For as heavy as the thing was, you'd think it would be fine, but it wasn't. It broke into pieces, and then"—her words sped up—"And I had already damaged his couch with the vacuum. By accident. But when Christian bumped into it, the leg gave way, and it collapsed, knocking a priceless painting from the wall."

The laugh snuck out of him before he could help it.

Derek had met Christian Strand exactly once, and the guy was a pompous asshole. He quite liked the idea of the other man getting smacked in the face with his own Oscar.

At the sound of his chuckle, a look crossed Pepper's face. Not hurt exactly—it was more like resignation—but he knew immediately that he'd done the wrong thing in laughing.

Pepper didn't give him the opportunity to apologize.

She stood, the chair's legs scraping against the tile floor.

"It was just the typical Pepper O'Brien disaster," she said lightly. "No lasting injuries, but my dad paid a settlement anyway and gave him his choice of projects."

She crossed to the counter, retrieved a metal bowl, and pulled out a piece of glass that looked to have come from the jar he'd broken earlier. She tilted it this way and that, staring at the transparent material as though it held state secrets.

Derek frowned, opened his mouth.

The piece dropped back into the bowl with a soft *clink*.

"Things worked out, I guess. The movie he chose is already getting Oscar buzz, and it's not even in full distribution yet." Her eyes found his. "So, there you go. The whole sordid tale."

"Pepp—"

"I'm going to take a shower. I trust you can show yourself out."

She disappeared down the hall before he managed another syllable. The bathroom door closed, the lock clicked into place, and Derek sat by himself at the kitchen table with two glasses of wine, both nearly untouched.

Who was the alcoholic now?

# ELEVEN
# MORNINGS SUCK (THAT'S WHAT SHE SAID)

Pepper

SHE WATCHED Rylie run toward the playground with cheerful abandon. Shannon dabbed her eyes, clearly the more affected of the duo on the first day of school.

"Thanks for coming," Shannon said. "When Brian didn't make it home—"

"Aside from being way too early," Pepper said, "I'm touched that you thought of me."

The bell rang, and Rylie ran to line up with the rest of her class. The parents were apparently allowed in for only a few minutes before they'd be booted by the teacher. Judging by Shannon's tear-filled gaze, that tactic seemed wise.

"Should I wait for you out—"

Shannon grabbed her hand. "Please come."

Okay then.

"Sure." They trailed the kids into a brightly colored classroom filled with miniature desks and the letters of the alphabet tacked along the ceiling. A carpet took up one corner, a reading area the other.

The space was peppy and fun and crowded with parents.

"Find your name," the teacher called.

Rylie zipped around the room, stopping only when she found her name at the aptly named Blue Table. Blue nametags dotted its surface, a blue pencil holder sat in the center of the five blue chairs.

"I love blue!" Rylie announced then she settled down to color a handout the teacher placed in front of her.

The woman was in her mid-forties and blond with a friendly smile. "I'm glad."

"Hi, Suzette." Shannon extended a hand. "I really should be better at this."

"Aw, it's okay," the teacher, Suzette, replied. "It's like this for all of us."

Pepper glanced around the room, looking at all the happy faces and parents trying to hold it together. She'd never had this.

A nanny had taken her to school.

And boo-hoo, poor rich kid—

"And you are?" the teacher asked.

She blinked, forced a smile, and extended her hand. "Oh, sorry. I'm Pepper. I'm just here for moral support."

"My daddy's at work," Rylie chimed in as she colored the sky, as one might have guessed, blue.

"Nice to meet you, Pepper," the teacher said then turned back to Shannon and whispered. "It's easier if you go sooner rather than later."

"You're right, of course." With a nod, Shannon bent to hug Rylie. "See you in a couple of hours, honey."

"Bye, Mommy!" Rylie chirped, returning the hug before continuing with her coloring.

Shannon held it together until she got out the door. Then she sniffed and a couple of tears fell.

"Coffee!" Pepper said. "STAT!"

"I-I'm fine," Shannon said, dashing away those tears.

"We need carbs and caffeine, immediately."

"I don't have time for coffee. I've got to get to my classroom." A shuddering sigh as she pulled out her phone to check the time. "The bell is going to ring in five minutes."

"Go on, then. Get your teacher hat on, and I'll bring you back lunch in a couple of hours."

"You don't have to—"

"I want to." Pepper bumped her shoulder and offered her a tissue. "I promise I won't even cook it. I'll play it safe and buy us some treats from the coffee shop."

That teased a smile from Shannon. "Okay, deal." She pulled Pepper in for a quick hug. "Thanks for . . . you know . . . helping me not freak out."

"Distractions are my specialty."

She waved and walked to her car. It only took a few minutes to drive downtown. Stoneybrook had a Starbucks, like basically every other place in the world, but the locals preferred Mocha's. The quaint shop had apparently been there for decades and though the outside had been spruced up, the inside was homey and warm.

Brown leather booths were spaced evenly along the far wall, and she slid into one. A waiter brought her a menu, and she ordered her drink and pastries.

Yes, *pastries*. Because carbs were everything.

Only after she'd scarfed down half of her food—a cinnamon roll and chocolate croissant were her choices for that particular day—did she realize that the waiter was standing at the end of her table.

He was an attractive boy, man, well, *boy* with closely cropped brown hair and green eyes.

She wiped her mouth and waited.

"I wanted to see . . ." He hesitated, glancing at his feet

before back at her. "I guess I wanted to see if you would want to . . . go out with me."

This exact thing had happened in her life far too often, honing her radar to a fine point. He wasn't interested in her. He wanted a way in the O'Brien dynasty. Which was unfortunate because it would be nice if this one with his tanned skin, muscular forearms, and a few days of scruff *did* like her. Hell, it would be nice if *any* man liked her without an ulterior motive—

Derek.

He seemed to like her. As a friend, of course. Or perhaps, a slightly confusing and very clumsy younger sister.

But still there was at least *one* man she could added to her list.

"What's your name?"

"Todd," he said.

"You don't have to ask me on a date to show me a script, Todd" she said softly.

His relieved breath made her. Feel. So. Awesome.

"Give it to me next time I come in," she told him, "and I'll—"

"I actually have a copy right"—he ran to the counter and pulled out a folder from behind the register—"here. I majored in English with an emphasis on screenwriting and . . ."

Pepper took the stack of papers and set it carefully beside her while Todd prattled on. Finally, she interrupted the excited boy—yup, definitely a boy—and asked for a refill.

"Of course! Thank you so much, really!"

"You're welcome," she said, pushing away her plate and placing some cash on the table. "Maybe I could get that refill to go?"

LATER, to-go cup in hand, script tucked under one arm, Pepper walked down Stoneybrook's main street. She'd stashed the screenplay in her car but couldn't bear to head back to her house. Not when it was quiet and lonely and—

Her brother was getting married.

Andy was the best man.

She had to play nice with her cheating ex and attempt to not ruin the wedding. Why did she have to? Why couldn't she tell her family to just screw off and not go to the wedding at all?

Because . . . she was still hoping they might change, that she could find some peace and happy and her place with them.

A snort. Truly, she had a better chance of a fairy godmother appearing out of nowhere and transforming her cut off jeans into a ball gown than finding her place within her family.

But she was still going.

The next step was escaping the wedding unscathed. Her goal was no broken limbs. Or blood. Or sharknados—

"Sunshine."

She didn't immediately stop, not recognizing the male voice or that the hail was in reference to her.

"Hey. *Sunshine.*"

Oh geez, she thought, turning to see a man quickly walking up to her, her spine going stiff, her eyes narrowing. What was he going to try to sell her on? Music? Another screenplay?

"Look, buddy," she snapped. "I'm just trying to walk here."

The man was a few inches taller than her with sandy blond hair and nicely tanned skin. His teeth flashed white against the pale pink of his lips. "I'm just—"

"I'm. Not. Interested." Pepper whirled away.

"You dropped your phone," the man said. Amusement clouded his tone.

Of course she had.

Sighing, chin dropping to her chest, she spun back around.

The man extended her phone. "Have a bad morning, sunshine?"

"You could say that," she muttered. "Sorry I took it out on you."

Broad shoulders rose and fell in a casual shrug. "It happens." He tugged on the end of her ponytail. "Judging by the red of your hair, I'm guessing you're this Pepper O'Brien everyone is talking about?"

She shored her spine, prepped for the next request that was certainly coming her way. "Yes."

"Cool," he said. "Your eyes are gorgeous by the way. They go perfectly with your skin."

Um. What?

Their conversation died off, awkward drifting in.

"Okay, well. Thanks?" She put her phone in her pocket and turned back in the direction of her car.

"Want to grab some coffee?" the man blurted.

Pepper raised her cup in answer.

That threw him, but only for a second. "Oh. Well then, how about dinner?"

"I'm"—she shook her head—"I don't even know your name."

He muttered something under his breath then gave her a smile that was really quite dangerous . . . in a bumbling, charismatic male sort of way. "I'm screwing this up. Rob Hansen." He extended a hand, the barest hint of pink drifting across his cheeks. "I'm newly back in this dating game thing . . . and apparently, sorely out of practice when it comes to talk with a gorgeous woman."

Pepper smiled, charmed despite herself. He was cute. Good-looking, unassuming, and not *too* perfect.

And, *God*, did her life need imperfect.

"Why are you only newly dating?" she asked.

A shadow crossed his face. "My wife passed last year."

"Oh, no. I'm sorry." She brushed her fingers lightly across his arm.

"Me, too."

And cue awkward, this time at Pepper's behest.

She took a breath, forced a cheerful smile. "Bert's burgers at six p.m."

Careful brown eyes touched on hers. "What?"

"Meet me tonight."

His head tilted. "Is this a pity date?"

"No! Of course not."

"It *so* is a pity date." One corner of his mouth quirked. "But I'll take what I can get. Nice to meet you, sunshine."

He turned and walked away.

"If you plan on wanting a second date then you'd better give up the nickname," she called.

He paused, tossing a wink over his shoulder in a way that was definitely *not* awkward. It was smooth and sexy . . . and maybe just a little dangerous. "I think you like it." Then he was gone, striding down the slate-covered sidewalk with loose-limbed ease.

Her breath caught at the sight. She'd never thought awkward had the potential to be sexy.

Apparently, she'd been missing out.

Shaking her head, she started back toward her car, lifting her cup to her mouth and taking a sip of the now lukewarm coffee as she walked—

Then tripped over a crack in the concrete.

Liquid dripped down her chin, cascaded over her shirt, staining the white material brown.

Sighing, Pepper tossed the cup into the trash.

Awkward. She knew *all* about awkward.

Unfortunately, she didn't think it was quite so sexy on her.

## TWELVE
# RED ISN'T JUST FOR BLOOD

Derek

HE WAS LEAVING STONEYBROOK.

He needed to hit the road early in the morning, to scout out the final town for his documentary. That was the only reason he was stopping at Pepper's place to take her to dinner.

He *needed* to say goodbye. Had to see her one more time before he left.

Idiot. This was dangerous. This was stupid.

But . . . that afternoon in her cottage, watching her fold in on herself because he'd laughed when she shared something painful and embarrassing. He'd been an ass. He should have told her she was strong and impressive, that he thought it was really cool that she was trying to make it on her own. That he respected the decision.

He hadn't.

And he hadn't been able to stop thinking about her, about the way she'd held herself as she'd walked away.

Like she was fragile.

He didn't want to be the cause of that.

Ignoring the warning bells in his brain, he bounded up the steps, raised his hand to knock, and—

The door swung open.

Pepper's head was down as she rummaged through her purse. "Where are my flipping keys?" she muttered, stepping across the threshold and colliding with him.

His hands came up, and he caught her shoulders.

She screeched, flailed.

Derek dodged an elbow. Her hair flew across his face. "Hey," he said. "*Hey.* It's me."

She froze. "Derek?" she asked, yanking her head back, strands of hair catching on the buttons of his shirt. "*Ouch.*" A grumble, one petite hand coming up to wrestle her locks free.

He watched her struggle, unable to help. Not when her body was flush against his, not when she smelled like vanilla and jasmine and . . . he inhaled, his body tightening.

Pale pink lips. Freckles on her nose.

His arms dropped so quickly that he had to raise them again to steady her.

He actually wanted to kiss the girl.

*Fah-la-la-la-la—*

"Jesus," he ground out, shoving down the pervasive film song while carefully putting some distance between the two of them.

"What are you doing here?" Pepper asked, one hand perched on her hip.

"I'm taking you to dinner," he said.

Which was going to be a lesson in sexual frustration, apparently. His eyes flicked down to his dick and he mentally ordered it to obey.

When he glanced up again, Pepper was staring at the very misbehaving bulge behind his zipper.

He waited.

And *waited*.

At least until the tip of her tongue darted out and ran across the surface of her bottom lip.

He coughed, raised a brow when her eyes met his.

The flush on her cheeks, the deep green of her irises didn't help his bulge-situation.

She visibly shook herself then reached into her purse again and pulled out a set of keys. After closing and locking the door, she faced him again.

"I'm sorry," she said. "I've already got dinner plans."

"Already—" Derek blinked, started after her when she breezed past him.

"Another time," she said. "I have a date."

His inner caveman really did *not* like that.

Especially when he saw what she was wearing.

A short—*too short*—dress that matched her eyes. She needed to put on a jacket. Or a muumuu or—

He relaxed slightly as he watched her cross to the next porch, climb the stairs, and knock. That cottage, he'd learned from their earlier beach day, belonged to Pepper's friend and daughter, Shannon and Rylie, respectively.

So it was a girl's night.

That was better. Except . . . he thought of Pepper going to a bar, of strange men approaching her and—

He shouldn't care.

He cared anyway.

Especially when Shannon opened the door and handed Pepper a pair of sky-high heels.

She'd break an ankle.

Pepper squealed and threw her arms around Shannon's neck. The action lifted the hem of her dress and drew Derek's gaze down.

For fuck's sake.

The woman had a spectacular ass.

"Tell you all about it later!" Pepper called and flounced down the steps. She stopped abruptly at the bottom, as though surprised he was still there. "Oh."

Oh?

Women were *always* happy to see him.

And oh?

Just. *Oh?*

"Rain check," she told him and started to walk by.

Derek snagged her arm. He *should* have let her go, should have left her to the date.

It was the lipstick that pushed him over the edge.

Fire engine red.

Fucking kissable.

He reeled her in, silky skin beneath his palms, soft curves against his chest, jasmine and vanilla in his nose.

He leaned down.

"Don't." A whisper. A plea.

His mouth was a centimeter from hers, and those four letters painted his lips. Moist breath. Hot air. She might as well already be kissing him for how effectively that puff owned him.

"I shouldn't," he agreed.

"You shouldn't," she agreed. Another breath, another chink in what was fast-becoming a non-existent resistance to Pepper.

His lips inched closer. "I want—"

"*No.*"

Those emerald eyes were brimming with heat, her skin was flushed, her body pressed against his.

But she'd said no.

And so he released her.

Pepper's eyes slid closed, shuttering that warmth, and she released a shaky breath. "I can't, Derek." A beat. "*We* can't."

His body was on fire, but he nodded.

Eyes opened, sadness in place of desire. The swap was a punch to the gut. "I could never be what you need."

Gripping the shoes in one hand, Pepper turned and ran barefoot down the beach.

She was gone so fast that she couldn't have heard him when he said, "I think . . . I think I just need you to be you."

# THIRTEEN

# CHOCOLATE ISN'T GOOD FOR EVERYTHING

Pepper

THANK GOD FOR WATERPROOF MASCARA.

And cold ocean breeze.

She paused by a bench just off the beach, ostensibly to slip on the heels Shannon had loaned, but really to catch her breath.

Dimples. A plump bottom lip. A hard body that felt too right against hers.

A man that would break her.

Into way more pieces than Andy ever had.

The heels were gorgeous . . . and leather death traps. But sometimes a girl had to risk all for fashion, and this was one of those times.

Pepper needed to feel pretty on her first date in forever.

The *click-click* of her high heels against the sidewalk paired with the hem of her silk dress teasing the outsides of her thighs did the trick. Concentrating on not murdering herself on the slightly uneven slate sidewalk cleared the rest of her mind.

Derek was out. Rob was in.

She strode into Bert's Burgers and enjoyed the fact that she didn't trip when every pair of eyes swung in her direction.

Granted, she *was* a little overdressed for the occasion—

"You look *amazing*," Rob stood just inside the door, clad in a pair of jeans and a polo shirt.

"This old thing?" She winked . . . or attempted to anyway.

Concern clouded his face. "What's wrong with your eye?"

Mentally rolling those eyes—because, really, she didn't want Rob to think she was having a seizure or something—Pepper forced a smile. "Nothing. Should we sit down?"

"Oh." He straightened, mock-bowed, and extended an arm. "Of course, milady."

That fake smile turned into a real one. The man was too much. "You're a dork," she said giggling. "Which is perfect because I am, too."

His eyes met hers. "And your laugh is beautiful."

Her breath caught. "I—" Words clogged up in her throat. She looked at him . . . really *looked* at him.

He was serious. When had fire-engine red hair and pale-as-hell skin ever been considered beautiful? Pepper was the living embodiment of a Raggedy Ann doll, and no one thought that patchwork of a mess was gorgeous.

"Come on," he said, tugging her forward.

Since words were still failing her, she followed Rob to a booth.

They sat on opposite sides of the table and stared at each other.

At least until he got up and crossed to her side. "Scoot over," he ordered.

She shifted toward the wall. He slid in. She stilled, waiting for it. Waiting for the heat to wash over her like it did with Derek, for goose bumps to spread over her arms, for her heart to squeeze.

It didn't.

Not even when Rob put his hand over hers and murmured, "Hi." She grimaced, he winced. "Too much?"

Pepper answered honestly before she could stop herself. "Maybe?"

A wry smile crossed his lips. He was cute and seemed sweet, but he wasn't Derek.

"I'll go back to my side in a minute," he said. "Just tell me two things first"—his eyes flicked over their shoulders—"Who's the guy glaring daggers at me, and was he the one who made you cry?"

She felt it then.

The slow burn of sensation as heat trickled from her toes upward, spread down her arms, through her torso. Pulse increasing. Insides knotting.

Derek.

"Why do you think I've been crying?" she asked instead of answering.

Rob rolled his eyes. "Because I was married."

"And marriage gives you the power to read minds?"

"No," he said. "But it did make me observant." He brought his hand up, touched the skin at the top of her cheekbones. "Reddened eyes. Flushed cheeks." His finger swiped the corner of her lashes. "A rogue tear. What happened?"

"I—"

"Pepper."

She'd felt Derek coming near.

Felt it just as effectively as a dog sniffing out bacon. Her body stiffened, flared to life.

She glanced up. Derek was glaring down at her. Well, he was being generous with that glare, and had extended it to Rob as well. "What?" she snapped.

"I need to talk to you."

Rob looked at her, raised a brow, but as cute as he was, she could hardly focus on him.

When Derek was near, it was hard to see anything else.

"Ah. I understand," Rob said. "I get it now." He leaned in to whisper in her ear, "Jump. Be brave and go for what you want. I'm so glad I did."

Before she could respond—hell, even as the meaning of his words was processing through her Derek-addled mind—he slid from the table.

"Rob—" she began and started to stand.

Derek sat down next to her.

Rob gave her a half smile. "See you around, sunshine."

She pushed Derek's shoulder. "Let me out."

"Why?" he snapped. "So you can chase after the man like a—"

"What will you have to drink?" a gruff voice asked.

Pepper called on every ounce of her patience to not sock Derek right in the jaw and smiled up at Bert. "I'm not staying, I'm afraid."

"She'll have a chocolate milkshake. I'll have a water," Derek said and before she could protest, Bert nodded and walked away, wisps of white hair swishing as he went.

"I'm not—"

"Hear me out."

"Why?" she crossed her arms when shoving at Derek's shoulder didn't budge him an inch. "So you can interrupt me seventeen more times?"

"It was one time if we're being precise."

She threw her hands up. "I'm never precise. I'm chaos and disorder and—"

"Color and life and—"

"Stop interrupting me!"

"You're stunning in that dress, Pepper," Derek said. "The

green matches your eyes, and your body"—he shook his head—"grown men are crying right now."

"And what?" She jerked her head in the direction of her chest. "Just because I have breasts now, you're interested in me? No, thanks. Go get another skanky conquest."

"That's unfair."

"You know *what's* unfair?" she asked. "You being as gorgeous and hot as you are. Dimples for God's sakes! Two of them is really overkill."

Those little indents made an appearance.

Her eyes narrowed and she waved a hand in the direction of his face. "See? They make women stupid and—"

"Your father wants me to keep tabs on you."

Outrage was such a bolstering emotion.

So much better than the humiliation that trailed through her at his words.

"Chocolate shake. Water." Bert plunked the glasses on the table. "Be back in a minute."

"Excuse me," Pepper said when he'd gone, pushing at Derek's shoulder again. She needed to get the fuck out of this restaurant. She needed—

"Pep—"

"Don't use that fucking name," she gritted. God, this was *enough*. She'd come to Stoneybrook wanting a fresh start. Instead, all she'd gotten were uncomfortable memories and painful slaps of reality.

She wanted, *needed* to escape. To forget this happened and—

"I'm—"

Fuck it.

She picked up the milkshake and . . . dumped it on Derek's lap.

With a curse, he jumped up, swiping at his crotch. Pepper seized her opportunity and rushed out of the booth.

Unfortunately, she went too fast.

Her spiked heel slid on the puddle of milkshake gathering on the floor, and she skidded, arms flailing, feet skating on the slick surface. And—

Down. She. Went.

# FOURTEEN
## I'VE GOT MY TIGHT PANTS ON

Derek

HE TRIED TO CATCH HER.

He really did.

Pepper still went down like a sack of bricks.

Her skirt flew up, and he shouldn't have looked. But he did anyway. And sweet Christ, her ass—clad in barely there black lace—jiggled in that perfect *female* way. The one that made him want to nip and kiss then slide around to her front to do the same there.

All of a sudden, his pants weren't cold any longer. They were painfully tight.

Martial arts. His grandmother's underpants. Water-borne illnesses.

Derek tried to think about anything except Pepper's glorious ass and how much he wanted to grab it.

Which was so *not helping*.

Pepper struggled to sit up, hands yanking at the skirt of her dress so fiercely he was surprised that she didn't rip the thing to shreds, but then the hem was brushing the middle of her thighs and Derek's brain began working again.

She kicked off the heels and stood, eyes closed, for a long minute.

Then they opened, her hand rose to her bra, she extracted a twenty-dollar bill, and placed it carefully on the table.

"Sorry for the mess," she told Bert.

And she disappeared.

Derek should have let her go. Left her to her troubles, let the complication that was Pepper O'Brien run straight out of his life.

He didn't.

He grabbed Pepper's twenty off the table and replaced it with two of his own. After an apologetic smile to Bert, he took the towel a waitress offered him and made his way out of the restaurant.

Chocolate ice cream dripped down his thighs, soaked into his socks.

His personal Hansel-and-Gretel moment. Only instead of breadcrumbs, he was trailing drops of milkshake.

Pepper had disappeared by the time he pushed through the door of Bert's Burgers. He spun, searching, expecting . . . to what?

Find her waiting for him.

Unlikely, after he'd bungled through the conversation about her father and ruined her date.

Derek started for her cottage even though it was somewhat unsatisfying not being able to chase after her like he wanted. Still, he had enough Millennial in him to realize he was being slightly unreasonable.

Only slightly.

Snorting, he dropped the towel into a trashcan and turned the corner for the beach. Cold air hit his crotch, and he winced.

Fuck, that was cold.

Almost as cold as Pepper's eyes had been as she'd left the restaurant. Though, that should be a good thing. His movie depended on him keeping her out of trouble . . . and though Paul hadn't explicitly stated it, Derek knew it was also equally dependent on keeping his dick in his pants.

His feet slid to a stop in the middle of the sidewalk as images bombarded his brain. Black lace, pale skin, pink nipples—okay the last was his imagination, but he'd had no shortage of that in his life as of late.

If he'd pulled his stopping routine in L.A. or New York, other pedestrians would have pushed past him, bumped into him, irritated that his moment of fantasy had interrupted their rush to the next important place on their to-do list.

In Stoneybrook, he was alone.

No one brushed by him. No one glared.

And he was stuck with disturbing thoughts coming to perfect clarity.

He was attracted to Pepper. Well, obviously. *Any* man or woman would be. She was gorgeous, and not only on the inside. As sappy as it sounded, she had an internal kindness that exuded from her pores, but Derek was also starting to realize that he didn't know her at all.

Poor Pepper. Klutzy Pepper. Train Wreck Pepper.

*That* was the girl he knew. *This* woman—still klutzy, still slightly chaotic, sexy and sweet and somewhat sad—was wrecking havoc on him in a different way.

Her father wanted him to watch out for her. *He* want to fu—

Well, suffice to say, his instincts weren't purely protective.

He wanted her. As a woman. Not a charge to keep track of.

And *that* was going to screw up his life.

Deliberately, he rotated, turning his back to the ocean and his front toward the bed and breakfast he was staying at.

He might have made it, too.

If not for the flash of red, the swirl of green coming around the corner, black heels in her hand, eyes down, emerald dress wet from the milkshake she'd dumped in his lap and plastered to her body.

"Pepper."

The shoes clattered to the sidewalk, but she didn't bend to retrieve them.

They stared at each other, frozen, unsure, until—and he would never be sure which one of them moved first—the distance between them was somehow gone and Pepper was in his arms.

"Why can't you just leave me alone?" she asked, a bead of milkshake dripping down her cheek.

He swiped it away. "Because every time I look at you I forget why I should."

Her mouth was right there. He leaned in—

She rose on tiptoe and slanted her lips across his.

Heat exploded along his spine, surged down, expanded until he was a blazing inferno. It didn't build slowly. It burst forth and consumed him. Her lips were like silk, her mouth sweet with the slightest undertone of mint.

And her body.

Soft breasts pressed against his chest, firm fingers gripped his shoulders, pelvis pressed forward to meet his own. They moved together, teasing, stoking the fire until—

Her mouth left his.

His heart raced. He couldn't get enough oxygen into his body, let alone to form words.

Pepper didn't seem to have the same problem.

"Goodbye, Derek," she murmured, before bending to pick up the shoes and disappearing from sight.

# FIFTEEN
## WHEN YOU THINK YOU HAVE THE WORST OF IT

Pepper

SHE DIDN'T GO HOME.

Or at least not completely.

She knocked on Shannon's door and when her friend answered, she promptly burst into tears.

"Oh, honey," Shannon murmured, throwing an arm around Pepper's shoulders and ushering her inside. "Come sit on the couch. I'll grab wine."

Pepper nodded, hands still gripping Shannon's killer heels as she moved to sit down.

"Here." Shannon thrust a box of tissues in her hands.

"Sorry," she sniffed, swallowing down the tears and trying to get herself under control.

"Take your time," Shannon said. "But at least tell me if I need to call the police."

That dried Pepper's eyes. "Police?"

"You're dress is ruined, you're limping, and your arm is all scraped up."

She glanced down, took in the beautiful—*ruined*—emerald

silk, the red marks on her arm, her swollen ankle. "Trademark Pep," she muttered.

"What?" Shannon asked.

"My date didn't hurt me. He didn't have the chance to even attempt it, considering that Derek crashed our table approximately two-point-two seconds after we'd sat down."

Her friend gasped, plunking onto the couch and setting a bottle and second glass on the coffee table. "You're kidding."

"Unfortunately not."

"I knew it!"

"You did not."

"Derek likes you Pepper. Anyone could see that."

"You're wrong," she said, even as her mind flashed back to the kiss. God, it had been good. No. It had been great. No. It had been the hottest kiss of her whole flipping life.

Which was just damn perfect.

Derek. Annoying, persistent man. Ruiner of perfectly average and acceptable kiss memories.

"I'm not wrong," Shannon persisted. "I know when a man wants—" Her eyes dimmed, smile becoming forced. "Anyway, anyone could see the man is crazy about you."

"He's here because my father is funding his next movie and asked Derek to keep an eye on me."

Shannon's mouth dropped open.

Pepper put her hand up. "And before you ask, I'm not guessing. He told me."

Her friend flopped back against the couch. "Well, damn. I thought—" She broke off again and cleared her throat. "Obviously, I'm no expert on men."

Pepper scoffed. "You've been married for a decade. I think you're doing better than I am."

"And look at me." Shannon's tone was so bitter that for a moment, Pepper was taken aback. "It's Friday night. I'm alone.

Just as I've been every other Friday night for the last twenty-two weeks. I know. *Because I counted.*" She swept her arm out. "Look. I've literally counted."

Pepper glanced around the room. The cottage was a mirror image of hers, a small, cozy family room, an open-concept kitchen with a small breakfast nook. Only Shannon's held toys and a play kitchen.

It had felt comfortable from the first time Pepper had visited for dinner—after two sandcastle-building play dates on the beach with Rylie. The couch was covered in a soft blue microfiber and a floral chair and ottoman took up one corner. Shannon had painted the wooden furniture white and given it a slightly distressed appearance. Shabby-chic, beachfront cozy, whatever a designer would call it, the home was . . . well, homey. Reality TV played quietly in the background, the wine and glasses sat on the table, but that wasn't what caught Pepper's focus. No, instead her attention was drawn to the day planner draped over one arm of the couch.

"Read it," Shannon said then rolled her eyes and started to reach for the little book. "Look at me. I've taken over the entire conversation and made it all about me." She tucked the planner behind her, shook her head, then reached for the bottle of wine. "Never mi—"

"It's fine. I—"

Shannon pulled out the cork and poured two glasses, but then she left them on the table as she stood and headed for the hall. "Let me get you some clothes. You have to be freezing."

Pepper snagged the planner.

A ribbon marked the date, and she left it there as she scrolled back through the pages. Rylie's activities made up most of the writing. Ballet class, swim team, Girl Scouts. But there were also lesson plans and . . . blue lines at the top of every page.

She squinted. No. They were really long arrows. That extended over multiple days.

The same four words repeated along each of them.

*Brian—out of town.*

Pepper blinked, flipped through more pages, more evidence of a life, of play dates and practices, of recitals and field trips.

And Brian out of town.

"I think he's having an affair," Shannon said when she came back into the room, her voice sad. "The man who was supposed to be the love of my life is having an affair."

Pepper's breath hissed out. "Are you sure?"

"Pretty damn sure." A pause as Shannon set a T-shirt and pair of sweats in Pepper's lap. "I got an email from a woman. With pictures—" Her breath caught. "Of the two of them."

"Oh my God. Who would do that?"

Shannon snorted derisively. "I know lots of people who would do that." She gave Pepper an arch look. "And I think you do, too."

Unfortunately, she guessed she did.

Shannon picked up the glasses and handed her one. "Now, enough about me. My life isn't going to sort itself out tonight, but I can attempt to help you with yours. So why don't you change out of those clothes and tell me how you ended up looking like a walking, talking milkshake?"

## SIXTEEN
# BEING DRUNK WOULD BE SO MUCH EASIER

Derek

HE WAS DRUNK.

He had to be. He *needed* to be.

Because otherwise he'd just blown any chance of a film career by kissing Pepper.

His phone buzzed just as she disappeared from sight. Gorgeous Pepper, womanly Pepper, the first woman to ever feel right in his arms Pepper. He took a step in the direction she'd disappeared, wanting . . . what?

"Fuck," he muttered. When his phone buzzed again he pulled it from his pocket.

Then promptly cursed again.

"Hi, Peter," he said after swiping his finger across the screen and putting the phone to his ear.

"Nice save," the older man said. Or rather barked, in his trademark O'Brien yell.

Derek frowned. "Save?"

"Getting Pepper away from that man," Peter said. "At first, from his background check, I thought he might be a good fit, since he was former military, but he was married before. To a dancer." Peter chortled. "And not the ballet kind. She was a backup dancer for a pop singer. My daughter couldn't be with a man who—"

Derek's mind cut away from Peter's ranting, and he couldn't help but wonder if Pepper knew that her father was scrutinizing her dates' pasts.

Probably not, he suspected.

Or *maybe* so. Maybe she rolled over like most people did when it came to the whirlwind that was Peter O'Brien.

Except . . . she was here. Attempting to get away from the O'Brien influence.

"—I'm calling off my men."

"What?" Derek asked.

"I'm going on a press tour for the next few weeks. They'll come with me."

"Okay, I'm leaving tomorrow for the next location. I'm sure Pepper will be fine. It's a safe—"

"No."

Derek had been turning in the direction of his hotel. Peter's stern tone made him freeze. "Sorry, what was that?"

"You heard me, son. Don't play dumb. You're staying in Stoneybrook."

"What about the—"

"If you want my money for the project then you'll do as I require."

Standing there, the clear night sky dotted with stars, the air slightly salty from the ocean breeze, sand gritting under his shoes, Derek almost told Peter to go fuck himself.

Then he thought of the rejections, the cool dismissals when he'd sought funding. He thought of his project and the value he might bring.

And he realized he was no different from anyone else.

Peter O'Brien had something he needed.

He was going to roll over and cave.

"How long is the press tour?"

"Two weeks," Peter responded, tone jovial again. "You get Pepper to fall for you. You keep her in line. Then you'll fly down on the jet with Pepper for the wedding." A beat. "Make sure she's not late."

Derek ground his back teeth together. "Fine."

"And son?"

He could only grunt.

"Don't forget flowers and jewelry. The way to any woman's heart is wasting a little money on trivial shit that doesn't mean anything."

Now *that* loosened Derek's tongue. "W-what?"

"Kissing only gets you so far. And this is my daughter we're talking about. If you're going to keep her in check, she'll require a certain amount of . . ."

"Finesse?" he couldn't help but fill in the blank.

"No. *Finance.*" Peter laughed at his own joke and hung up.

Derek mechanically slid the phone into his pocket and thought of Pepper's small cottage on the beach, of her mismatched chairs and worn cushions.

She didn't seem like a woman who wanted expensive flowers or a diamond bracelet.

She came across as normal. Sweet. Kind.

And he was more confused than ever. She'd responded to his kiss, but not in the way he expected. She'd pushed him away. Told him no on the beach.

Except, she'd kissed him back.

For one brief moment, she had kissed him back.

And it had been glorious.

Desire for Pepper warred with his need to see his project through. This, Peter wanting him to make Pepper fall for him, was completely wrong. But . . . it wasn't like he didn't want her, and not just because her father was pushing him in that direction.

Derek liked her. A lot.

So what would be the harm?

This was a fucking dangerous slope to be sliding down.

"*Fuck.*" He turned and slammed his fist into the brick wall of the building, pain exploding up his fist and arm, reverberating through his fingers.

He was a fucking idiot. He couldn't do this. Even if Pepper was beautiful and intriguing and wonderful. He needed to cut ties with everything to do with the O'Briens. They were toxic. Pervasive and—

Pepper.

The sadness in her eyes. The smile that had curved her lips when she'd played with the little girl on the beach. Her in that dress, sinfully tight. Her lips against his, her body pressed flushed to his.

He wanted her.

And . . . he was a moron.

He shook out his aching hand as he walked to the bed and breakfast, flexed his throbbing fingers when he talked to the registration desk about extending his stay. Dunked the swollen limb in the ice bucket as he tried to figure out what to do next.

All he knew was that he couldn't stay away.

It would torpedo his career if he did.

And his heart—

Aw. Fuck. He couldn't go there.

# SEVENTEEN
## CHEESECAKE HEALS ALL HURTS

Pepper

SHE WAS PLEASANTLY tipsy when she walked the ten feet from Shannon's cottage to her own and as such, nearly killed herself on the package sitting on her doorstep. Luckily, she was back in bare feet, having left Shannon's death trap heels back where they belonged.

Still, she grunted in pain when she tripped over the box, scrambled to not trample it, overcorrected on her sore ankle, and ended up colliding hard with the doorframe.

"Well, that's going to leave a mark," she muttered, bending carefully to pick up the small cube of cardboard.

And when she saw the label, she was extra glad to have not squashed it.

Her phone rang, and she would have known who it was without the *Star Wars* ringtone.

Only her father would call so late.

Only her father's spies would tell him the exact moment she'd gotten his gift.

It almost made her want to chuck the cheesecake to the deck, the way he kept tabs on her.

Except it was cheesecake.

Carefully, she set the box on her patio table and extracted her phone from her purse.

"Hi, Dad," she answered.

"You're welcome for the delicious and expensive delivery, Father."

Just that quickly, annoyance swept through her. She bit back a frustrated sigh. "Thank you for the cheesecake. It's my favorite."

"It cost more than its weight in gold."

She flopped down onto a chair and tilted her head back toward the sky. The stars were always so bright here, so much more than in Los Angeles.

"I didn't ask you to do that, Dad, but thanks," she said.

"Well, no need to be snotty," her father said. "I just wanted to spoil my daughter."

And lord it over her.

She opened her mouth to snap out a reply then just as quickly closed it. Nothing she said would make one lick of difference anyway. There were so many other important injustices—starving children, natural disasters, terrorist attacks. No one gave—or should give—a damn about her irritation over a flipping cheesecake.

*It didn't matter.*

She chanted that to herself over and over as her father continued to talk. Not that the notion made her feel any better. Derek's name booming over the airwaves and colliding with her eardrums snapped her out of her inner diatribe.

Derek of the soft lips, flat abs, and hard—

"He's *what?*" she shrieked, finally processing her father's words.

"Going to escort you to the wedding."

She shot to her feet. "He is *not*."

Her father's eye roll was practically audible. "Yes, he is. The man is working for me. I need my security guards for the press tour, and you need someone to watch out for you."

"I don't—"

"You could do worse than Derek. He comes from a good family. His background is squeaky clean. He knows the business."

"And it always comes back to the business," she said, knowing her voice was bitter yet unable to stifle it. "Doesn't it?"

"The business gave you . . ."

Off he went.

Pepper got it. Her family had given her a lot, and she wasn't ungrateful. Or didn't mean to be anyway.

She just kept circling back to wanting something different.

Why was it so bad to dream of a small life?

Her existence didn't need thousand-dollar shoes and Maseratis to be worthwhile. These few months at the beach had been her happiest ever. If only she had a way of making some money.

Then she could suck it up and excise the toxic—A.K.A. completely cut ties with her family.

She dug through her purse and pulled out her keys as her father prattled on. A quick second later the door was open and her purse was on the little table she kept in the front hall.

His voice never faltered as he regaled her with the reasons she was so lucky and ungrateful.

He wasn't wrong. Or not entirely.

She was both of those things in that moment.

After grabbing a fork from a drawer, she went back onto the deck and opened the box.

Low. Fat.

The cheesecake might as well have been laughing at her.

Her father had bought her *low-fat* cheesecake.

Figured.

She closed the lid, set her fork on the table, appetite suddenly gone. Judgment and strings. Why did there always have to be so much judgment and so, so many strings?

Strings for gifts. Strings for favors. Strings for affection.

They wound around her, tightening, siphoned off her air.

"Now don't eat all of that in one sitting," her father said, proving her other thought about so much judgment. "It's low-fat, not calorie-free, and the dress that your mother chose—"

"I'll see you at the wedding." She hung up.

Hearing her father's voice suddenly cut off made her feel slightly better. The low-fat cheesecake sitting on her table did not.

With a huff, she scooped the box and fork up and went into her house.

The container made a satisfying *thunk* when she dropped it into the trash.

After swapping the fork for a spoon, Pepper grabbed a pint of ice cream from the fridge and dug in.

Full fat with chocolate chunks and bits of brownie mixed in.

Fit into her dress.

For God's sake.

The worst part was that her father still got to her, even though she'd tried to lock that part of her life away for months now. She wished that she could be one of those people who could *live and let live*.

That wasn't her.

She brooded. She thought and thought and *thought*, dissected every single detail, thought about all the ways she could have done things differently.

And nothing changed.

Nothing *ever* changed.

With a sigh, she put the ice cream back into the freezer.

She walked over to the sink, dropped the spoon inside, and rested her hands on the counter, staring out the window to the dark beach beyond. The *swoosh-crash* of the waves just barely reached her ears.

"What are you going to do with your life, Pepper?"

Hollywood was out. Once, she might have made an okay actor, perhaps even a semi-successful one. But that was gone, and she'd never loved it anyway. It had been another way to prove herself, to show her family she could contribute to the O'Brien success.

She could go back to school.

Except she didn't like school much anyway and was she going to spend even more time getting a degree that didn't matter?

Maybe she could get her teaching credentials.

Except kids and a classroom full of scissors and pencils was basically a time bomb of ways to injure herself or them.

Or worse, she could teach teenagers.

Shuddering, she let her head flop back.

Or rather, started to let it fall back.

Because as she moved, her eyes stopped on a reflection. On the same sparkle that had caught her attention when Derek had broken the jar a few days before.

Wood. Glass. Shells. Sand. Steel.

Derek. Her father. Andy. Weddings that were supposed to have been hers.

She grabbed the container and dumped it into the sink. The pieces clattered together, glass broke further, shells chipped.

And it all somehow made sense.

String. Glue.

Her hands moved, but not as fast as her mind.

A piece of glass there. A shell with twine here. The wood was the base and the other parts somehow just came together.

The sky was lightening when she finished. Pepper held up the small sculpture, watched little rainbows of the sun's rays reflect through the glass and throw rainbows onto the bright white shells.

Somehow it all made sense.

How? How did it make sense?

And yet, her pain and hope for the future had been encapsulated on the washed up chunk of driftwood.

She felt lighter. More whole, despite the pieces she'd put on that wood.

She didn't care about her father and his judgment or his strings quite so much.

Carefully, she set the sculpture on the window sill, watching it for a minute more, seeing it sparkle, broken yet still hopeful, and with a satisfied smile on her lips, she turned and left the kitchen.

Sleep took her away the moment her head hit the pillow.

# EIGHTEEN
## ALWAYS GO FOR THE EXTRA WHIP

Derek

HE STARED at his laptop screen for what seemed like an eternity.

Even if he sold his share in the family business, invested every drop of his savings into the project, he still couldn't afford to make the documentary.

"Coffee?" A male voice intruded on his mental calculations. "You had the large black, right?"

Derek nodded and took the outstretched cup. "Yes, thanks. Sorry, I was zoning."

"If I was looking at spreadsheets, I would be, too." The man extended a hand. "Brian."

"Derek." Why did that name sound familiar? "Thanks for grabbing that."

He studied the other man, took in the sandy blond hair, the pale blue eyes, and medium build. They *could* have met before, but there wasn't the slightest bit of niggling recognition. It was just the name—

"Daddy!"

Both of their heads whipped toward the sound, and Derek watched Rylie run across the floor of Mocha's. He wouldn't have believed it, but the café's coffee was a definite step up from the chain places.

Rylie threw herself at Brian's legs and latched on tight. "Hi, baby," he said sweeping her up into his arms. "I missed you."

"I missed you, too!" Rylie said, taking her dad's hand and tugging him toward the counter. "Adriana at school has a new puppy, and I learned how to write words with S-N blends and I . . ."

"Hi, Derek," Shannon said.

He turned from the scene. It took the barest glance into Shannon's eyes to realize she was upset. Shadows darkened the skin under each, and she looked exhausted.

"Are you okay?" he asked in an undertone.

Her eyes flicked to the cell in her hand and back to his. She'd already looked at it a handful of times since she'd walked in.

"In solidarity, I shouldn't even talk to you."

Derek's gut went tight. Obviously she knew about the catastrophe that had been his interaction with Pepper last night.

"But I think you two could be good together."

"That's—" He wanted to say impossible, instead he settled on, "not going to happen."

"It could." A sparkle of mischief entered her eyes. It was much better than the sadness of the previous moment. Unfortunately, that sparkle only lasted a second. Then her gaze drifted over to Brian and Rylie, and all the life drained out of her face.

"What's wrong?" he asked.

She looked down at her phone again as Brian went to grab his coffee. "Pepper's not here and not answering my calls. She was supposed to watch Rylie so Brian and I could talk."

That sounded ominous.

It also had him offering, "I could watch her for a few minutes." If only to take some of the strain from her expression.

Knight on white horse complex. Check.

"I couldn't—"

"Mr. Derek!"

"Hi, Rylie." He smiled and put his palm out for a high five. "How're the sandcastles?"

"I built one with a turret yesterday, and my mom dug a moat and oh!" Sharp six year-old eyes spied his cell. "Can I play your phone? Do you have Angry Birds?"

He grinned and unlocked the screen. "I don't. But I have Minecraft."

"I love Minecraft!"

Most kids did . . . as did thirty-year-old men.

Rylie grabbed the phone and plunked down into the booth next to him.

He bobbed his head at Shannon. "We'll hang out until Pepper gets here. She's not flakey. If she said she'd come, she'll be here."

"What if she's *Peppered* herself on the walk?"

His lips twitched. "If she doesn't show in a bit, we'll go look. Plus, she's got your number. I'm sure she just got held up."

A thread of worry crept into him, but he pushed it away. She was fine. Probably just upset and tired, but fine.

"Hey." Brian returned to the table, coffee in hand. Derek noticed that he hadn't bought one for Shannon. "I didn't realize you knew my family."

The emphasis on *my* made Derek's hackles rise.

"I'm friends with Pepper," Derek supplied anyway. Shannon was Pepper's friend, and he didn't want to make things uncomfortable for her. "We grew up together."

At the mention of Pepper, Brian's stance relaxed. "The klutzy redhead? Has she always been such a mess?"

"Brian!" Shannon chastised. "I—"

"You wanted to talk?" he said, words clipped out. "I've only got a few hours to get stuff sorted before I fly out—"

Shannon's expression clouded. "But I thought you were going to be home for a few days. The disposal isn't working, and I think the washer is leaking."

Brian shrugged. "Call a repairman. God knows with as many hours as I've been working we can afford one."

Derek watched the exchange closely and as thus, he saw Shannon's eyes slide closed for a beat, felt her hurt at the dismissal as palpably as he would feel his own. What kind of jerk was Brian to not see that his wife was upset?

"Looks like a booth opened up," Derek said, pointing. "Why don't you take it?"

"Oh." Brian glanced over. "Nice." He turned and headed for it without a backward glance at Shannon, whose shoulders slumped heavily.

Derek had the feeling she saw Brian's back way too often.

"Can I buy Rylie a hot chocolate?" he asked and stood. "And you a latte? Or tea?"

"I can—" She reached for her purse.

"Shannon!" Brian called the same time Rylie cheered, "Chocolate!!"

"I got it," Derek said. "You can buy me a cup next time. What do you like?"

She rattled off an order and hurried over to the table where Brian sat.

"Want to hang out here?" he asked Rylie. "Or come up and order?"

"Stay here," she murmured, eyes on the screen.

Derek smiled and walked to the counter to place the order. He watched Rylie as he waited for the drinks, her mouth moving as she concentrated on the game. That little girl was cute, had a good personality, and plenty of spunk.

"Careful," he said when he came back to the table and handed her the hot chocolate. "Don't burn yourself."

She took a careful sip. "It's only warm."

"Good." He raised the second cup. "I'm going to bring this to your mom, okay?"

"Okay!" Except it sound more like "shmo-kay" since Rylie's mouth was practically glued to the opening of the plastic lid.

Derek tried not to listen when he approached Brian and Shannon's table. He still heard:

". . . I've got the email right here, Brian. And she included pictures."

"It's bullshit. I can't believe you're going to come to me with this now. I'm leaving in—"

"You're *always* leaving."

Derek made his footsteps loud enough that he would rival a herd of elephants. "Thought I'd return the favor." A forced smile as he handed the cup over to Shannon. "Your coffee was up."

"You like coffee?" Brian asked, brows pulled down. "Since when?"

"Since always," Shannon said and took a sip.

Derek backed away, but not before he heard her say, "Though it must be tough to keep up with all the little pertinent details when there are multiple women in your life."

He slid back into his booth just as Pepper burst into the coffee shop. Her hair was frazzled and she wore pajamas. Her gaze flew around Mocha's until it collided with his.

The force of those green eyes took his breath away.

She was so fucking beautiful.

He could also read her mental debate from twenty feet away.

She was late, supposed to be watching Rylie. But she also wanted to be nowhere near him.

Duty or avoidance?

Duty won out.

Pepper walked over, feet dragging. "Hi," she said.

"Pepper!" Rylie's eyes flashed up and then back down to the phone. "I'm playing Minecraft."

"You don't say," she said dryly.

"White chocolate mocha?" he asked. "Extra whip?"

Yes, he knew her order. No, it wasn't pathetic.

Okay, fine. Yes, it was pathetic.

Her mouth dropped open. "Uh—I . . ."

Derek stood up. "Keep an eye on Rylie, okay?" And he made his third trip to the counter.

This time he returned with a plate of pastries to go along with the drink. Judging from the exchange at Shannon's table, the conversation didn't seem to be going well.

They might be there a while.

Though, now that Pepper had arrived, he could leave.

He *could* leave.

He could get up and walk right out of the coffee shop and put this tangled mess of money with conditions, of hopes for a future away. He could go back to the firm and work the system, find loopholes, garner settlements.

He could.

He didn't want to.

There was no freedom in that. No fresh air. No small town relationships. No need to know coffee orders or kids' names or when school started.

His previous life was fake.

*This* one was real. It was full to the brim with hurts and hopes and possibilities and failures, but it was real.

And it had Pepper.

Who said things like, "I could seriously kiss you right now."

# NINETEEN

# PASTRIES AND PUPPY DOG EYES

Pepper

IDIOT. She was a big ole idiot. With extra cherries on top.

Derek's blue eyes darkened. His lips parted.

That little gap of open space was enough. Enough to remind her of the feel of his mouth against hers, the strength of his arms wrapping tight around her. His smell. The cool touch of ocean air. The rough slate beneath her bare feet.

Need swept over and through her, twisting her insides, causing wetness to gather between—

Rylie's giggle snapped her out of her mental porno.

"You said kiss," the little girl said..

Pepper's cheeks went molten, but she had grit, dammit. So she forced her lips into a semblance of a smile and ruffled Rylie's hair.

"It's just an expression, sweetie." A wave toward the plate of deliciousness—carbs, chocolate, cherries, more chocolate, and more, *more* chocolate. "Usually uttered when someone brings me chocolate."

Rylie, who was sporting a hot chocolate mustache herself,

nodded in agreement. "My mom said it when I shared my ice cream with her."

"That was nice of you," Pepper said, dutifully ignoring Derek. His expression had darkened.

"I *am* really nice. My teacher . . ." Rylie was off and running, reciting some exploit of helping pass out papers and sharing crayons. Aside from an "Uh-huh" here and there, she didn't need much of an active conversational partner.

Which was good.

Because Pepper's eyes—traitors, the both of them!—had drifted over to Derek.

Anti-dimple-gate.

As in, they'd disappeared, and the frown he was sporting was intense.

Seriously though, why did dark and broody have to work on him? Hmm? Wasn't it bad enough the man was attractive when he was smiling? Why did the universe feel the need to add exceptional brooder to his freaking resumé?

"And you kiss a lot of people?" he asked.

Pepper blinked and sat back. His tone was dark, deadly, and as such, it took a moment for his words process.

Her chin lifted. "Why would it matter if I did?"

Now was his turn to blink, to sit back slightly shocked. His words, when they eventually came, were along a different vein altogether. Confused and frustrated, with a hint of resignation. "It wouldn't." A pause. "It *doesn't*."

Her reply was out before her better sense could stifle it. "I think you mean it *shouldn't*."

They stared at each other, both acknowledging the truth.

An underlying attraction connected them.

But they weren't going to pursue it.

No. Matter. What. Except . . . why did those feel like famous last words?

Pepper grabbed a pastry off the plate and shoved it in her mouth.

"I need to go." Derek shoved his laptop in his bag and stood. "Hey, kiddo, why don't you save your game? That way next time I see you, you can continue on."

"Okay," Rylie said and handed him his phone after a few presses on the screen.

"Bye—"

"Will you come to my school social?" she asked Derek when he turned to go. "My dad is going to be working. Again," she added with an expression that was equal parts hangdog and genuinely sad.

One Pepper had been taken in by more than a few times.

Oh, man.

Derek, like any tough, alpha male when exposed to the depressed eyes of a skilled manipulator (aka a six-year-old), folded like a bad hand at a blackjack table.

"When is it?"

"Tomorrow night at six of the clock," Rylie said. "My class is singing and then afterward there will be ice cream!"

Her little tush wriggled in excitement on the booth.

Pepper smiled and when she looked over at Derek, his lips were twitching, too.

"Well I can't miss ice cream, now can I?"

*Crack.*

She actually felt the defenses she'd erected against Derek sustain that break. It was dangerous—*he* was dangerous—but dammit if he wasn't a good guy.

Jerks were so much easier to write off.

Derek with his rescuing her from getting smooshed by cars and humoring a little girl he barely knew wasn't as easy to dismiss.

But . . . he was also being paid by her father to keep an eye on her.

So yeah, *that* was an important fact to remember.

"Yay!" Rylie shoved past Pepper in the booth and launched herself at Derek.

A colder woman than her would have been unmoved by the sight of him carefully hugging the little girl in return.

She, on the other hand, was a puddle of goo.

"Bye," he murmured as she clamored back over Pepper and into the booth then picked up a Danish.

"Bye," Rylie said, waving.

"Pepper."

She glanced up at him, and their eyes held. Totally not fair he could do that, especially after he'd gone and busted through her defenses by being all sweet and kind.

"Dammit, why can't you be a jerk?" she snapped.

White teeth flashed, a low chuckle slid across the space between them, trailed down her spine, coated her skin.

*Eau de Derek.* Confident and sexy and an aphrodisiac all in one.

"I'll work on that, okay?"

And then the man did the most confounding thing. He cupped her jaw and ran one calloused thumb over her cheekbone.

He was gone the next instant, and she would have thought she'd made the entire gesture up—delusions of grandeur, or rather, delusion of *Pepper*—if not for the way her skin tingled.

Her freaking nerves knew Derek was different.

Which made her . . . Screwed. Yup. With a capital S.

Rylie turned to her. "You'll come, too, right?" Wide blue eyes, gently sparkling with unshed tears.

Oh yeah, Pepper was well aware that she was screwed.

# TWENTY

# WHEN EARS BLEED

Derek

DEREK FELT EXTREMELY conspicuous as he stood outside the elementary school and waited for Rylie and company.

A single man staring at kids as they walked into a school.

Oh yeah, there was no way that could go bad.

He'd come early, thinking that since the event started at six, he'd need the extra time to get a seat or something.

Apparently, he'd underestimated the school crowd's on time tendencies.

At six on the dot, Shannon and Rylie came around the corner.

But where he'd expected two, there were really three.

Pepper's arm was around Shannon's waist and Rylie held her mom's hand on the other side.

Shannon had the grim determination of a woman who was pushing through something completely unpleasant in order to put on a brave face.

Dark, almost black circles under her eyes, pale skin, disheveled hair.

Apparently the talk with Brian hadn't gone well.

"Derek!" Rylie shouted when she saw him. "You came!"

"I couldn't miss ice cream," he said, carefully returning her hug when she wrapped her arms around his waist. Rylie was fragile and breakable, and he was way too big and gangly. He could hurt her just by breathing wrong.

"I'm so excited!" Rylie shouted as she did a little dance and ran ahead. "See you in there, Mom!"

"Stage fright, she does not have," Shannon said with a rueful smile.

"You okay?" he asked.

Pepper shook her head violently.

He frowned. What the heck was wrong with asking someone how they were doing?

Shannon sniffed and her eyes filled. A little sob hitched in her throat. "Brian never—"

Pepper grabbed her shoulders and shook her slightly. "Not here," she said fiercely. "Rylie is waiting inside, and you don't want to be a red, puffy mess when I take a thousand pictures of you and your daughter later, okay?" She reached into her pocket and shoved a tissue at Shannon. "Wipe your eyes. Take a deep breath. And buck up. Your kid needs you."

Shannon took a deep breath. "You're mean." But she was smiling. "Also, thank you. I needed that."

"Wine. Ice cream. Tears. Later."

"We're already going to have ice cream."

"So?" She shrugged, her red hair swishing around her shoulders. "We'll run it off tomorrow."

"I hate running."

"We'll pretend to run." Pepper bumped her shoulder. "Now come on, you're just being difficult."

Shannon took a breath. "I know. I feel like pouting and stamping my foot on the ground."

"We can do that later, too."

"True."

Derek was watching the exchange and trying not to laugh. He'd never really seen the fierce side of Pepper, and he thought that Shannon was pretty lucky to have a friend like her.

"If you two are done plotting then maybe we should . . ." He waved a hand at the school where kids were pouring in.

They jumped and screamed, running around like the little maniacs they were. The sight made him smile, almost as much as the two women in front of him starting when he spoke.

They'd forgotten he was there, but he wasn't offended. A person often learned a lot more by being quiet rather than dominating the conversation.

This time had been no exception.

Pepper was a good friend.

He'd known about her big heart and generous spirit. He'd been unable to miss the klutzy, troublemaker.

But she was so much more than that.

Shannon gave him a sheepish smile. "I guess we should go in, huh?"

He nodded. "Yup."

"I hope you two are ready for some off-key singing," she said.

Derek smiled. "Off-key singing sounds perfect."

---

Derek was rethinking his statement not twenty minutes later.

Kindergarteners had the rare ability to sing at ear-piercing levels. Or maybe it was shrieking?

Either way, his eardrums had to be bleeding.

Wincing, he rubbed cautiously at one and the action caused

Pepper to glance over. She smiled. A genuine one that made him feel seven feet tall.

"Thank you for coming," she murmured, leaning toward him while turning back to face the kids. They stood at the front of the auditorium on risers, singing their little hearts out—or most of them did. Some were sitting down, others were picking their noses, a few were shoving their neighbors. Cacophony was really the only word for it.

And at the center of it all was Rylie. *She* wasn't partaking in the nasal cavity searching, but rather, was singing her little heart out as she danced and wiggled in place.

How could her father miss it?

He shrugged when Pepper glanced over at him again. He hadn't answered her, found that he couldn't force any words as anger swept over him.

This little girl might not be hurting now, might not understand the context of an absentee dad.

But she would.

Someday she would.

A memory of Pepper popped into his head. It had been her birthday, her sixteenth or seventeenth, he couldn't remember exactly which. He'd been in college, pre law school, but the LSATs had loomed heavily over him. Paul had coaxed him away from his studies for the afternoon, and he'd been disappointed by the gaggle of girls clogging the pool.

His vision had been drinking a couple of beers with some friends, hanging out poolside, then watching the football game.

Seventeen, he realized. Pepper would have had to have been seventeen, because it had finally been legal for him to drink those beers.

He had hidden in the pool house, beer in hand, as Paul and the other guys had joined the pool party. Laughter and splashing competed for the top noise. Then had come the big, booming voice of Peter O'Brien.

*"Everyone gather up. It's time to sing Happy Birthday to Pep!"*

*That commanding tone had been enough to pull Derek out of hiding. He'd walked out just as the song began.*

*"Happy Birthday to you . . ." The group sang as Peter held a large cake just a few inches away from Pepper's face where she gripped the pool's wall, her head and shoulders above the water, while her body remained in. Candles flickered and danced, and it seemed like an awfully precarious location for baked goods.*

*The last notes rang out, and Peter extended the cake. "Make a wish."*

*Pepper stilled, eyes closing. Her hair was wet, darkening the bright red to auburn. She wore an emerald swimsuit that Derek thought was a close match to her eyes.*

*Her eyes had always stood out to him. Open, brilliant green, and—*

*"Cannonball!"*

*Paul.*

*Pepper's lids flashed open, her lips parted . . . just as a wave of water crashed over her and the cake.*

*Peter dropped the platter and jumped back as water splashed onto the pool deck. Plunk went the confection right on to Pepper's head and chest. Frosting melted, slid into the pool, a cloud of purple and pink dye spreading through the water. The candles fizzled out.*

*"Wicked!" Paul said as he swam over to his sister and scooped up a dollop of frosting. "Yum," he said, sucking it into his mouth.*

*Then he swam away laughing as the girls shrieked and scrambled to get out of the pool.*

*Of course, the guys were willing to help, chuckling and copping an extra feel here or there as they "assisted" the girls from the pool.*

*All except Pepper.*

*Who still clung to the wall.*

*Peter cursed. "Always you, Pepper. This always happens to you."*

*"I—"*

*He scowled. "Now I need to change for my meeting."*

*"But I thought you and I were going to watch the new film tonight."*

*"We did? Hmm." Peter ran his hands down his suit and made a sound of disgust. "Italian silk. Ruined." Then he turned and walked for the house.*

*When Derek turned back to Pepper she was gone. A flash of green emerged from the opposite side of the pool, a sheet of red hair dripping down her back as she pulled herself out.*

*She wrapped a towel around herself and disappeared into the pool house.*

*Paul and the guys laughed and joked with the girls, the party having moved to the Jacuzzi.*

*Derek took a step in the direction of the pool house. He should check on Pepper, make sure she was all—*

*"Grab me another beer, D," Paul called.*

*He hesitated a beat then turned away from the house. Pepper probably wanted to be alone. He snagged a couple of beers from the cooler and walked over to the Jacuzzi.*

*After handing the bottle to Paul, Derek found himself being coaxed into the hot tub and then soon after with a giggling girl on each thigh.*

*Not a bad place to be, all things considered.*

*And later, when they finally pulled themselves from the water, Derek remembered Pepper.*

He'd gone to check on her, but she had been nowhere to be found.

# TWENTY-ONE

# TOO MUCH ICE CREAM IS ACTUALLY POSSIBLE

Pepper

"GREAT JOB, KIDDO," she said when Rylie came bounding over after the kindergarteners had finished their song selections.

"I sang loud."

Uhhh. Yes, this was true.

"You sure did, sweetheart." Shannon held out a jacket. "You cold?"

"No. I want ice cream!"

Shannon smiled and tucked the jacket under her arm. "Okay."

Rylie squealed and ran outside of the auditorium. She seemed to have already scoped out the ice cream situation because she sprinted directly to the tables where bowls and cartons of deliciousness were set out.

Whipped cream. Cherries. Sprinkles.

Faster than Pepper thought possible, Rylie had a bowl full to the brim and was pounding ice cream like a champion competitive eater.

And just like someone shoving down sixty-something hot dogs, Rylie's face went green.

"I don't feel . . ."

Shannon reacted to Rylie's tone in a heartbeat, snagging the ice cream and tossing it into a trashcan before having Rylie take a few deep breaths.

"My tummy—"

She heaved.

Shannon brought the can in front of Rylie's face so quickly that the Flash would have been impressed.

Deftly, she caught her daughter's hair and rubbed her back gently.

"I'm sorry, baby," she murmured. "Do you think you're finished?" she asked when Rylie stopped.

A nod.

"Okay then, let's get you home."

Shannon tucked the jacket around Rylie and tugged her close to her side. Rylie was crying softly, apologizing between sniffles.

"It's okay, honey." Shannon gave an apologetic smile to Pepper. "We need to go."

"Do you need any help?"

Shannon shook her head. "We'll be fine. Too much ice cream too quick." She started shepherding Rylie back toward the parking lot then stopped all of two feet later. "Shoot. I forgot to grab my bag from the classroom. I left it earlier and I need—"

Rylie moaned.

Shannon hesitated. "Forget it. I'll grab it tomorrow."

"I can get your bag," Pepper said. "Just tell me where it is, and I'll bring it by later."

"I don't want you to—"

"Mom," Rylie said pathetically. "I want to go home."

"It's okay," Pepper said. "Let me help you."

Shannon bit her lip.

"I'll go with her." Derek.

Pepper wished she could say that she'd forgotten he was there. Except that would be a lie. Her body knew whenever he was close. He was the gold coin on the beach, and she was the metal detector. A low level *beep-beep-beep* always in the background.

And that beeping was growing louder.

His chest was close to her back, his voice brushing her ear. She shivered.

Shannon glanced between them and smiled. It was the first happy gesture Pepper had seen on her friend's face since her conversation with Brian.

"Room seven." She rifled through her purse and extracted a set of keys, tossing them at Pepper without warning. "It's the blue key." Pepper reached for them, somehow managing to catch the set or, rather, bobble with it long enough that Derek managed to snag it from her grip.

By the time she looked up, Shannon and Rylie were gone and Derek was smiling down at her.

"Room seven?" He held up the keys, blue one extended.

"Sure," she muttered, knowing there was no point in arguing with him.

Plus, he had the keys.

"Lead the way, sweetheart."

She stopped, glared. "I'm not your sweetheart."

Derek was unaffected. "We can stand here all night, or we can get your friend her bag."

Pepper sighed, but she turned in the direction of Shannon's classroom and started striding across the blacktop.

"Are we going to talk about it?"

The kiss? Her father? The fact that she was attracted to him? *Ugh.*

"No." To all.

"How about why you were late to watch Rylie?"

Now that question made her stumble. Okay, stumbling wasn't unusual for her. She couldn't blame her klutziness on words, but she sure as hell could blame it on Derek startling her.

"I overslept." Which was the truth. Or rather, a version of it.

Pepper wasn't ready to share what she'd been spending her days (and nights) doing. She was raw inside, knew it was too soon for her to tell if it was actually something.

If, for once in her life, she wasn't screwing something up.

Derek glanced down, studying her for several heartbeats. "You're not lying."

"And you think"—she stopped and plunked her hands on her hips—"You think you know me so well that you can tell when I'm lying?"

He smiled, dimples popping out to wink at her and no— dammit, *no*—her stomach didn't tremble the slightest. Not. In. The. Slightest.

"Yes," he said. "I do." Then he raised one brow, daring.

"I'm a virgin."

His mouth dropped open. He took a step toward her, tripped, and had to throw his arms out to steady himself. *"What?"*

He could tell when she was lying. Ha. Yeah, not so much. Also—thank you, sir— she plucked the keys from his hand and walked away.

Or tried to.

A hand on her waist stopped her, pulled her back against a hard chest. His spicy scent surrounded her. His heat soaked through the thin cotton of her blouse. Derek leaned close, hot breath puffing against her neck. "What do you mean *I'm a virgin?*" he growled.

She almost moaned, just barely stopping the sound by biting her tongue.

Hard.

"*You're* a virgin?" she asked in mock-surprise. "I never would—"

"Pepper." Her name was ground out, masculine frustration mixed with something else. Concern? "I give. I'm sorry."

*Drip. Drip. Drip.* There went her barriers against him again. Only this time they were melting. Disintegrating into useless puddles of nothing. Or maybe that was just her.

"Let go," she hissed, pushing against his arms. "There are kids around."

"Where?" Derek murmured. He gripped her hips, slowly turning her in his arms until she faced him. His eyes were hot. "We're alone," he said. "So, no, I'm not letting you go. Not unless you really want me to."

Pepper's breath caught, and she glanced away, taking in the empty hallway, its lights dimmed, its walls decorated with bright construction paper projections, a line of cubbies along one side.

She catalogued the floor. The sliver hinges of the handles and hinges.

She looked anywhere but Derek's gaze.

Because she *didn't* want him to let her go.

And that was dangerous.

"Pepper," he murmured, voice a velvet rasp that slid down her spine.

Suddenly, there was nowhere *but* Derek's gaze. Her eyes flicked up, seeing that he watched her, and intensity clouded the space between them, almost palpably coating her skin. She squeezed her thighs together when a bolt of heat arrowed downward.

He noticed.

*Of course* he noticed.

His eyes flicked down then back up. To her eyes. To her mouth.

"I'm going to kiss you now." One hand cupped her jaw, angling her head. "We'll talk later."

"I—"

His lips slanted across hers. She dropped the keys.

A movie song.

His kiss was that ballad at the end of happily wrapped up romantic film, the hero and heroine's lips touching as fireworks exploded, the movie cutting to black on a tranquil happy ending. It was sweet and coaxing, gentle but then it turned hot, all-encompassing . . . and it threatened to take her to her knees.

Because Derek had her.

He. Had. Her.

But he didn't want her—or not just her. He wanted her name, her family connection. He wanted . . . something she couldn't give him.

Panic gathered in her toes, the slightest little tapping of her foot against the floor. It spread up to her legs, her torso, her arms and hands, unclenching her fingers from his hair. Finally, it reached her brain and the emotion was a scalding brand. A hot poker that had her wrenching her mouth from his.

"I-I can't," she said, chest heaving.

Derek's breathing wasn't any steadier. "Why not? Why can't we have some fun while we're both stuck here?"

She bent and picked up the keys from the floor. "Putting aside the fact that you're babysitting me for my father, that"—she waved a hand—"is exactly the issue."

"*What* is?"

Pepper shook her head as she walked over to the locked classroom. "You want just fun." She inserted the key and turned the handle. "I don't do casual sex, Derek. And I definitely don't mess with my dad's lackeys."

He trailed her into the room. "I'm not—"

"You're working on a project with him. *That's* why you're here." When he didn't reply right away, she turned and walked toward Shannon's desk. "You don't have to answer. I already know." A sigh. "It's the only reason . . ."

"Reason?"

She snagged Shannon's bag and tossed it over her shoulder. "Look Derek—"

"I'd have to be an idiot to not want you." He took the bag from her.

"I can carry—" She sighed, saw a stubborn expression cross his face, and forced herself to not argue about the stupid satchel.

"I want you," he murmured. "Just you."

Except, he didn't. Look. She knew she wasn't a troll. She was fit—somehow despite her chocolate and wine addiction—and had a pretty face. But it was the rest of it. *All* the rest of it.

The infamy. The disasters in her wake. The overbearing dad.

"Tell me you're not here only because of the contract with my father," she said. "Tell me you aren't staying in Stoneybrook because he ordered you, too."

Tell her. Please tell her.

Because she wanted it to be true. For someone to want her just as she came . . . even though she knew that it wasn't going to be the man standing in front of her.

"I—" He cursed, shoved his free hand through his hair. "It's not that simple."

Her heart sank even though she knew it shouldn't—she'd warned the damn organ after all.

"It *is* that simple," she said, tucking away the pain, bolstering her walls, protecting herself. Because . . . she had to. If she wanted to finally move forward, to start truly being herself, and to become a strong person who didn't just wilt when her family or the world was unkind, then she had to buck up and start acting like one.

"Pepper—"

"You wouldn't be here if not for a project. My father has you over the barrel." She crossed to the door and flicked off the lights. "I get it. No hard feelings. My dad has a lot of pull in Hollywood, and I know you've left the law firm."

"*Pepper.*"

"If you want to get a movie made, he's your man," she went on. "So I won't make it difficult for you. You can babysit me. Just don't spout bullshit about how beautiful I am or how I'm so hard to resist."

"I—"

"Come out so I can lock up."

Derek sighed but walked from the classroom. "That's not how it is."

She locked the door and turned to face him. "Then tell me precisely *how* it is. You wouldn't benefit from a relationship with me? My father didn't push you into anything? After all these years, you've suddenly *seen* me and I'm the woman of your dreams?" She brushed past him. "Two truths and a lie. And I damn sure know the lie."

When Derek remained silent, Pepper shook her head. "Just leave it be. No more kissing. We'll play nice until the wedding, and then you're off the hook."

She yanked the bag from his hand and began walking down the hall.

"I never knew you to be so jaded."

A shrug. "One could say that you never knew me at all."

# TWENTY-TWO
## THE PLAGUE

"SO WHAT DO YOU THINK?" she asked Shannon. "Is it horrible?"

Her friend had slipped over that evening to pick up her bag after Rylie had finally crashed. Poor thing was really under the weather. Pepper hadn't wanted to keep her friend, but she also couldn't stop herself from asking Shannon's opinion.

On her artwork.

It felt strange to even say that.

She appreciated art, had the trust fund that meant she could buy a gallery's worth. But she'd never thought to make some of her own.

Shannon silently studied the piece of driftwood, glass, and shells, and Pepper began panic-talking. Which happened when she desperately didn't want to care about someone's reaction and yet she really did, and then she couldn't stop words from blurting out and she ended up filling the air with all sorts of nonsense. "I wanted to add some sea glass but I didn't have any and I think it kind of looks cool with the sharp edges and stuff. Of course, it wouldn't work with kids around. Someone might get cut and—"

"Pepper?"

"Yeah?"

"Shut up."

She clamped her lips together.

Shannon plunked her hands onto her shoulders. "It's gorgeous."

All of the pent up air escaped her lungs. "Yeah?"

"Yes," Shannon said. "You need to sell these."

"I—" she shook her head. "I didn't make it for that."

Shannon squeezed her shoulders before dropping her hands. "Which is precisely why it's so gorgeous." She snapped a picture with her phone before walking to the front door. "I've got to get back, but I'm sending this to my friend Mitch. He owns a gallery in San Francisco and that"—a nod to the sculpture glittering in the low light—"deserves to be on display."

"But—"

"Shh."

She sighed. "I was just going to say—"

Shannon glared, turned for the front door. "No arguments," she said. "I'm tired and my heart hurts and that is beautiful and—"

Pepper tugged open the wooden panel when Shannon faltered. Then she hugged her friend. "I was going to say thank you and"—she pulled back—"and I'm so sorry your heart hurts. And that I owe you wine and more ice cream."

Her friend sighed, hugged her back. "Yes, you do."

"Also, let me know if you need me to watch Rylie tomorrow while you're at work. I don't mind," she added when Shannon started shaking her head. "Should I turn the *no arguments* rule back on you?"

"No," Shannon said with a chuckle. "If I don't get whatever plague Rylie has, I'll take you up on the offer."

"Deal."

After another hug, Pepper closed the door.

Then she washed her hands. No plague for her, please and thank you.

---

LATER THAT NIGHT, Pepper decided she might have been better off dousing herself in hand sanitizer or jumping through a cloud of disinfecting spray.

Soap and water clearly hadn't been enough.

She spent the early hours of the morning heaving her guts up and then the next few camped out on the bathroom floor anticipating doing the same. Finally she crawled into bed and lay miserable and exhausted until the sun was high enough in the sky she could text Shannon.

PEPPER: *I've caught the plague. Can't babysit.*

SHANNON: *I'm so sorry! Do you need anything? So far I'm immune.*

PEPPER: *Lucky you. But no, I'm done with the puking stage. Now I want to sleep.*

SHANNON: *K. I'll check on you later.*

SHE TOSSED her phone onto her nightstand and closed her eyes, letting sleep drag her under.

It felt like less than ten minutes later when someone knocked on her window.

She glanced at her phone, saw it was past three in the afternoon. There were a half dozen texts stacked on the locked screen.

Shannon must be worried.

Pepper was almost too tired to care. Her mouth felt like a desert, parched and aching for liquid. Her head spun from the lack of food and fluids. Another knock on the window made her groan. At least her blinds were closed for a change. Sitting up made her head spin faster, and she immediately flopped back down onto the mattress. It was a struggle to reach her phone, but she managed to snag it from her nightstand. She'd text Shannon rather than getting up.

But just as she was typing, she heard the front door rattle and open.

The spare key. Of course.

"I'm fine," she called. Or rather, croaked. "I still have the plague, though, so steer clear."

"I'm not worried about the plague."

That hadn't been Shannon's voice.

She used her last remaining strength to toss a pillow over her head. Suffocation had to be easier than this.

The pillow was plucked from her face.

She kept her eyes closed.

"Pepper."

Derek was here. Why in the God was he *there*? Hadn't she made herself clear yesterday?

"Go away," she said, voice so rough it was barely discernible.

A cool hand brushed across her forehead and she almost moaned in relief. She was on fire and that cold touch was everything.

"You're burning up."

"I'm fine," she croaked. "It's just a bug."

"Sweetheart—"

"Shh." Her head pounded, her eyes ached. She closed them, and the lack of light was so much better. But when Derek didn't answer, she struggled to open her eyes back up. He was gone. Typical.

Except . . . she'd told him to go. So, she might as well take this time to sleep.

But now she was awake.

*Miserable* and awake.

What she needed was tea and a bucket of aspirin. And then for her body to keep both down. But she was too tired to do more than lift her head off her pillow.

*Come on now, Pepper. Woman up.*

Turned out she didn't need to.

The clatter of dishes on her nightstand drew her focus.

"What—?"

"Here." Derek slid an arm around her shoulders and tilted her up. Pepper hissed out an uncomfortable breath. Even though he was being gentle, the touch still made her skin throb. "Sorry," he murmured and stuck a few pillows behind her back so she was propped up.

"It's okay," she said hoarsely, having seen what was on the bedside table. Her mouth absolutely watered for . . . dry toast, a glass of water, and a bottle of aspirin.

"Shannon was worried," he said as he reached for the glass and tilted it up to her lips.

"She's sick?" Pepper whispered after taking a small sip. Even that burned.

"No. Said something about impressive teacher immune systems and how avoiding the plague was her superpower."

Pepper snorted. It hurt, but at least her friend's snarkiness made her smile.

"After you wouldn't answer her calls. Or mine, for that matter," he added, brows pulling down into a sharp V. "She was concerned that you were hurt. And since she couldn't leave Rylie, she sent me." He made a little salute. "Derek Cashette. At your service."

She frowned.

He grinned. "And no, that service won't be leaving you alone. You need food and liquids."

Since the word "food" made her insides squirm, Pepper just shook her head.

Derek put the glass on the nightstand. "Apparently Rylie is fully past the upheaval stage. Step one, according to Shannon, is keeping down water."

Pepper nodded, throat beyond done with the talking thing.

"And, in the mean time, we'll have a discussion."

She rolled her eyes.

"Okay, *you'll* listen and I'll talk."

Her mouth opened, but he placed a finger to her lips, apparently unconcerned about the dangers of spreading the plague.

"I talk. You listen."

She shook her head, eyes narrowing, but unable to find words. It would have been nice to say it was because of her sore throat. In reality, though, it was the feel of his skin against hers that really unnerved her.

She liked it.

And that was a huge problem.

Derek sat on the side of the bed, one foot on the floor, the other bent inward at the knee. Getting cozy, coming close, and she liked that, too.

Awesome, her multitude of problems were growing.

"Okay," he said. "I'm talking. You're listening."

"You've said that," she grumbled, albeit quietly. "Twice." A beat. "No, three times."

One side of his mouth curved up, a dimple flashing. "I guess I have." He sucked in a breath, released it slowly. "But here's the thing, Pepper. You unnerve me."

*She* unnerved *him*?

The man with the double dimples, the flat abs, and squeezable pecs was unnerved?

Ha.

But before she was able to voice her disbelief, he continued. "I need to be totally straight with you. Yes, your father is producing my pet project. Yes, he ordered me to stay here and keep you out of trouble. To watch out for you and—" He sighed. "I should have said no, but . . ."

Her father was a tough man to say no to.

"I didn't want to."

Her brows pulled down and, *ouch*, even frowning hurt.

"I like you, Pepper O'Brien," he said. "You're funny and so beautiful that it takes my breath away. I know that's cliché—"

Her stomach clenched, the water of the previous minutes suddenly churning like a whirlpool.

"—but I've always noticed you." He laughed. "Ever since that baseball bat collided with my head when we were kids, I've noticed you."

She swallowed hard, throat burning.

"I didn't tell your father no because . . . well, I wanted the excuse to spend more time with you."

Pepper covered her mouth, tried to push up from the bed, away from Derek.

He grabbed her arm. "Hey, Pepper. I'm—"

And . . . that was the moment she lost the battle with her insides.

# TWENTY-THREE

# I'LL WASH YOUR BACK

Derek

HE DIDN'T TYPICALLY MAKE women puke with his romantic sentiments.

Well, he didn't typically *make* romantic statements. But still.

Pepper groaned and stumbled away, slamming a door behind her. Sounds of retching filtered through the pane of wood.

He crossed over, knocked. "You okay?"

Her only response was a moan and more retching.

"I'm coming in."

"No!"

Ignoring her protest, Derek turned the handle and stepped into the bathroom. He filled a cup with water, wet a cloth, and turned on the shower.

When it seemed like the worst of it had passed, he handed her the cup with orders to "Swish and spit, not drink." Her hair was tangled and sporting some serious disarray, so he carefully brushed it off her face then wiped her forehead with the damp towel.

"Okay?" he asked when she released a breath.

A nod.

"Good." He reached his hands under the hem of her shirt and started tugging up.

Barely an inch of her ivory skin was exposed before her hands began flapping like a chicken, shoving him away, grabbing at the cotton material like it was a life preserver and she was going down on the Titanic.

"What are you doing?" She smacked his hand when he reached for the shirt again.

"No offense," he said, trying to bite back a smile. "But you smell."

The way her face cleared, went immediately blank made him regret the words. He could practically see the barbed wire being erected.

"I didn't mean that like it sounded," he began.

Her smile was forced, and she reached for the toilet's handle. "Doesn't mean it's not true." A pause. "I'm going to take that shower now." When he didn't move, she waved a hand at the door. "You can leave."

"And let you pass out? Crack your head open?"

She closed the toilet lid and gingerly raised herself up to sit on it. He'd never seen a person's skin look so gray. "I'm fine."

"Sure you are."

Derek didn't move.

Pepper sighed.

And he was struck again by how much he liked this. Bickering with her, just being with her. Watching her eyes flare with fire when he'd pissed her off.

It was so much better than the distance she kept trying to erect.

"Why don't you go?"

He told the truth. "I can't."

She groaned, in frustration this time rather than discomfort. Or maybe it *was* discomfort because what the hell did he know?

"I won't look," he told her. "But I'm not leaving."

"You—" A huff. "I— *You're*—"

"Wasting water," he pointed out, knowing that for the former California girl—where droughts were all too prevalent—the notion would get her moving.

And it did.

Though the glare she tossed his way should have unmanned him. Instead, it had rather the opposite effect on his *manly* part.

*Ew.*

That was a bad innuendo, even in his own mind. But Derek would be lying if he said that he didn't want to yank her close and demonstrate what he could do with that particular piece of his anatomy. However, since it seemed like a stiff breeze could push her over, he refrained.

Instead, he covered his eyes with his palms and attempted to not peek through his fingers like a child as she undressed.

He *attempted*.

Also, he didn't succeed.

Which turned out to be a good thing because not only did he catch a seriously spectacular view of some Pepper side boob, he was also watching closely enough to see her waver as she tried to raise her leg over the lip of the tub.

He moved in a heartbeat, steadying her before she went ass over teakettle into the shower.

Her eyes flashed to his. "You said—"

"I lied."

Fully dressed, he gathered her naked body close to his chest and stepped into the shower.

"Derek!" she gasped then moaned as warm water sluiced

over them, wetting his jeans and soaking into his shirt. "That feels nice."

He shifted so she was more securely positioned in the stream, trying not to remember that this was the third time he'd been sporting uncomfortably wet jeans in as many weeks.

Jeans that were also growing tighter by the second.

Because even though Derek was trying to ignore her naked-ness, to be a gentleman and help her since she was sick, he couldn't pretend she didn't do it for him.

Luscious curves. Deep red hair. Pale skin that was turning pink under the water's heat. The same pink he could imagine spreading over her body as he licked and teased and caressed—

Soap. He needed to get her clean and get out. Before he totally lost it.

But even having a purpose didn't help.

Her skin was like velvet, soft and dewy beneath his finger-tips as he spread body wash over her stomach. He further attempted to disregard the rosy pink of her nipples, the buds tightening beneath his touch.

It didn't work.

Her breasts were lush enough to make a weaker man—and he was one sappy Hallmark commercial away from turning in his man card, as it was—cry. Her hips, her ass, hell, even her pinky toe was adorable clad in soapy bubbles.

She was fucking magnificent.

And his body knew it.

Somehow he managed to make it through that shower.

Pepper, however, wasn't doing quite so well. Her eyes kept sliding closed, and she leaned more heavily against him. By the time he rinsed the shampoo from her hair, she was nearly limp.

"You okay?" he murmured, worried that she was going to pass out.

Come on, of course he'd catch her. But passing out was surely indicative of a bigger issue than a stomach bug, right?

"Fine." A sigh. "Tired."

"Okay," he murmured, checking her hair one last time for shampoo. "Almost done."

When it was completely clean, he turned off the shower and wrapped a towel around her.

Newsflash. Drying wasn't any better of a process for his libido.

But he was able to get her dry and in fresh pajamas. Though —heaven help him—not in any sort of respectable undergarments. One look through that drawer filled with lace and color and *black* fucking silk and he'd been done for.

"Thanks," she murmured as he tucked her back under the blankets. Fresh sheets probably would have been a good idea, but he had no idea where they were and he'd already dripped over the floor enough.

"Anytime, sweetheart."

Her hair was already drying, curling up around her temples. She looked about ten years old, innocent to the Nth degree. Of course that was until he saw her lips, lush and soft and pink, the way sunlight sliced over her cheeks and highlighted the bones there. Delicate, strong, a juxtaposition that confused his mind and heart.

He'd turned to leave the room—in search of a dryer for his clothes—when she asked, "Why are you here?"

A pause as he decided whether or not to put her off.

"The truth," she said.

Emeralds. Her eyes were spectacular green emeralds. But they also pierced straight through him, pinned him in place.

Derek crossed over to her, kneeling at her side next to the bed. "Does it matter?"

No hesitation. "Yes."

Shit. He'd been purposely not investigating his motivations too closely. He knew she was gorgeous, his body couldn't let him go a moment without reminding him, but the rest of it, the emotions swirling under the surface, the uncomfortable truths that he didn't want to think about . . . that was the part he didn't necessarily want to face.

"Your father—"

He stopped. Because it was just that. Yes, he was between a rock and a hard place when it came to financing the film, but this wasn't about that. His mind, *hell*, his heart knew that much. A strand of her hair was creeping forward, tickling the outside of her eye. He carefully brushed it back.

"Derek."

He sighed then admitted, "I'm trying to put into words what I feel in my heart."

Pepper's mouth formed an O and it was all he could do not to kiss her, stomach bug germs be damned.

"Every time I see you, a hundred memories flash through my mind. Summers at your house. This"—he touched the scar bisecting his right eyebrow—"demonstrating your lack of baseball skills. White string bikinis. And then I remember cannonballs by the pool, ruined birthday cakes, extinguished candles . . ."

Emerald hardened. No, that wasn't the right word. The softness was still there, just hiding beneath a layer of steel. Protected. Ensconced within.

And if that wasn't Pepper to a T, the Pepper of now, the one he'd discovered since coming to Stoneybrook, then he didn't know how else to describe her. She was all of those things. Strong with sweet. Tough with vulnerable.

"You feel sorry for me," she said cooly.

"No," he said then decided on full disclosure. "Okay, that *used* to be part of it."

More layers. More armor being erected, and . . . he was seriously fucking this up. He'd blame it on the damp jeans and wet underwear. Chaffing was not his friend. Except—

"It was all so much simpler when *that* was my life," he said. "When all I was interested in was parties and lawsuits and making as much money as quickly as I could, fuck the consequences. So yes, it *was* easier to ignore you." He brushed his knuckles across her cheek, watched as her eyelids slid closed. "I could ignore the pull I felt every time you were in the room, the pretty way you blushed, the laugh that slid down my spine and made its way into my heart. But then things changed and . . ." When her eyes didn't open, he went on. "Everyone always dismisses you, but I see the *real* you. I understand that you're more than you seem and . . . and I like you, Pepper. A lot." A beat of quiet. "I think actually . . . I think I may be falling for you."

Silence.

Slow and steady breathing.

He'd unloaded his heart and—

A soft snore.

Pepper was asleep.

Awesome.

Quietly, he pushed to his feet and walked from the room.

Two minutes later, he was naked, wrapped in a towel, and his clothes were in the dryer.

But not even the draft beneath it could distract him.

He'd bared his feelings, and Pepper had fallen asleep.

Clearly, he was losing his touch.

# TWENTY-FOUR
# THAT MILK, THOUGH

Pepper

HER EYES FLEW OPEN, and she rolled over to her back the moment Derek left her bedroom.

He'd said he was falling for her.

Derek Cashette said was falling for *her*. For Pepper O'Brien, black sheep of the O'Brien clan.

It just didn't make any sense.

He was rich, handsome, successful, charming. She was . . . a walking talking train wreck. So she'd done the only thing she could. Feigned sleep. Okay fine, so that wasn't the *only* thing she could have done. Maybe talking, responding, saying something as gorgeously and perfectly romantic back. Now *that* would have been so much better.

Except, again . . . it just didn't make sense.

Sighing, she turned the details over in her mind. Tried to understand it. But the pieces didn't fit. It was trying to push a puzzle piece into a slot that wasn't the right shape.

Derek Cashette being interested in her. Did. Not. Fit.

And self-flagellation much?

Why did she always do this to herself? Why was it so impossible to think that Derek might possibly be interested in her? She was a nice person. She didn't scare young children.

Or at least not often . . . and definitely not on purpose.

"Okay," she muttered to herself, rolling over onto her back. "And what if he really means it?" Her thoughts spun as she tried to understand her own emotions. Did she like Derek? Like really *like* him?

Pepper grimaced. One more like and she'd be back in the Valley.

Derek *was* hot. That was fact. One her body was well aware of. He was also nice, had always been the kindest of her brother's friends. But, he dated models. How did she stand a chance against *models*?

Her mind drifted back to the shower, to the erection that had pressed against her as he'd washed her hair.

Okay, so on the most basic terms possible, he was attracted to her. But what about the rest of it? Her father. The film. His baby-sitting. Yet suddenly those hiccups seemed much less important.

Derek liked her, and . . . she liked him back.

Carefully, she sat up. When her head didn't spin, she slipped from the covers and stood. Steady. No spinning room.

Check. Check.

The door was open a crack, and she paused before leaving the bedroom, listening hard. Had he left?

But no, she heard the rumble of the dryer just off the kitchen, a soft curse as something clinked in the kitchen.

"Suck it up, Pepper," she whispered and strode into the hall.

And if her footsteps slowed to a crawl outside the kitchen then that was just because the sight of Derek standing in nothing more than a towel as he raided her fridge had frozen her in place.

She must have made a noise.

Hell, it was probably a gasp. His body clothed was one thing. His body in just a towel . . .

Holy pigs in a blanket.

For once, his dimples were the last thing on her mind. Or at least the ones that graced his cheeks, err, his *northern* cheeks. The ones winking at her from the top of the towel, hinting at the bite-able ass beneath? *That* set was definitely front and center in her brain.

He spun around and—freaking rainbows, kittens, and cotton candy—the front was as good as the back.

And the towel. She sent out a mental thanks to the universe for that puny excuse of a towel.

Long limbs, a V above his hips, flat abs, a squeezable set of pecs.

Hers. Grabby hands all day long.

"Pepper?" he asked, face clouding with concern. "Are you—?"

No words. Her tongue wasn't capable of them at the moment. Not when it was glued to the roof of her mouth. Not when every nerve in her body had come to screaming attention and was demanding that she launch herself at him.

But she managed some self-control.

She didn't jump Derek or mark him, didn't stake an obvious claim to the universe that he was hers.

She was a lady. She had restraint.

Instead, she closed the distance between them and snatched the towel from his waist.

See? Control.

Then Pepper glanced down. "Oh."

One of his hands shot out, covering himself with a carton of milk. "It's drafty in front of the fridge. Cold—"

Pepper didn't let him finish. Because her *oh* hadn't been in disappointment. No, the exclamation had been one of reverence. The man did it for her. *Everywhere.*

Stomach bug? What stomach bug?

Weak? Hell no, she wasn't. Or not any longer, anyway.

Her blood pumped, adrenaline surging. She could lift a car, a building.

The pitiful restraint she'd managed before was gone. *Now* she launched herself into Derek's arms. He caught her, stumbling back a step and colliding with the refrigerator door. "Oh," she said when he cursed. "I'm—"

His mouth captured her apology and, if she was being honest, her heart.

Childhood crush turned into something more.

Pepper might not understand fully why he was there, couldn't comprehend why he was interested in her, but she also didn't care so much anymore. The ride. She was willing to go along with it.

To see where it led.

And—her breath caught when he stroked his tongue along hers—it seemed to be leading in a very pleasurable direction. Derek's hands slid up her waist, fingers teasing the outside of her breasts before stopping to rest on top of her shoulders.

When he tugged her a few inches away from him, disappointment speared through her.

Too much. Too fast. Too much Pepper and not enough finesse.

"I—"

"Shh," he said. "My ass is freezing. That's all."

She laughed. She had to. It was either that or cry, and she felt close to crying. *Way to go, Pepper. Assault the man who said he was falling for you. And while you're at it, have a go at freezing his gibbly bits.*

But before she could go too far down the self-pity rabbit hole, Derek swept her up into his arms.

"No," he said. "Cut out the bullshit that's running through your mind. Stop thinking whatever it is that's putting this look on you face." He nipped her bottom lip. "This isn't about the past. This isn't about our families. This is about us. Just us." He started walking from the kitchen. "Which means, I'm going to take you down that hall, give you an orgasm that's going to make you scream, and then hold you while you sleep the rest of your sickies off."

"Sickies?" she asked, and if she sounded breathless, it was because she *was* breathless, dammit. When he got all growly and demanding . . .

She shivered then released a shuddering breath when he grazed her throat with his teeth and whispered in her ear, "Okay?"

"O-okay."

An orgasm from Derek and not her plastic vibrating friend sounded like pretty much the best thing ever.

He swept them from the kitchen, cuddling her close, rendering her stupid as she got a front row view of that chest. And the way he smelled—fuck, she *loved* the way he smelled.

Spicy and male, a hint of pine in his aftershave. Tart and tangy and wholly Derek.

The man could bottle the scent, sell it for millions on the black market. *Eau de Dimples*, the fragrance that makes women stupid and melts their panties from their bodies.

"What are you thinking about?"

Her cheeks flared at his question.

"Nothing," she said. "My mind was just wandering."

Blue eyes flashed down. Amusement filled their depths, but it was the flash of dimples on Derek's cheeks that broke her.

"You smell good," she blurted. "And I want to rub against you like cat nip."

Humor darkened, shifted to desire. "Rubbing can be arranged."

"Derek!"

"Come on," he announced and plunked her down on the bed. "That was perfectly sixth grade in execution."

Flash went one dimple. Melt went her heart.

"I like you," she whispered. "I'm worried it might break me when this is all said and done." She gave in and ran one hand through the hair on his nape. It was silky smooth against her palm. "But I do like you very much."

"Sweetheart—"

His tone was soft, gentle as a mother handling a newborn. And that wouldn't do.

Her and her big mouth. She wanted passion, desire, *heat*. Not pity that she'd elicited herself.

Derek knelt on the bed next to her. Still naked, still gorgeous, but only half-mast.

Her words were killing the erection she very much wanted to become familiar with.

And that just wouldn't do.

So, her hands found his shoulders and tugged hard. In that one movement, he was on top of her, all hot skin and hard muscles, and if she had her way, hard in other places too.

"Kiss me," she ordered.

## TWENTY-FIVE
## WHO'S SICK?

Derek

HE NEEDED TO SLOW DOWN, to regain control. He needed to lock up his desire and focus on pleasing Pepper.

But he was finding that harder to do by the second.

Her mouth was against his, her body supple and sweet. She smelled like the rose-scented body wash he'd slicked on her skin. And even just the memory of being in the shower with her, of seeing her wet and pliant and—

His cock was an iron brand.

And it very much wanted to make friends with Pepper.

The rest of him wanted to mark her, to claim her as his own. To slay her enemies, flush away the hurtful past, pleasure her within an inch of her life.

Except she was still ill. Or at least recovering from it.

She didn't need him thrusting over her, exhausting her. Not when he could please her in so many other ways. Not when his pleasure could wait. Her palm slid down his arm, over his midsection, farther still until it wrapped around his hardness and stroked. Then *his* pleasure didn't want to wait, and when she twisted her wrist in some crazy hand acrobatics, it *couldn't* wait.

He. Couldn't. Wait.

It had been too long and—

*Control.*

"Derek," she moaned, wrenching her mouth from his and writhing against him. "I need. I—"

"Shh." His shush was calm while his insides raged, and that was probably abundantly obvious as he wrestled with her pajama pants. He tore them from her legs while thanking God that she wasn't wearing any underwear. He barely had the thought that he should be thanking himself for that particular gift, since he'd dressed her after the shower, before his eyes drifted down.

*Fuck.*

Mouth watering for a taste of that soft pink, he dove between her thighs.

His tongue worked her without mercy, teasing and flicking, pressing firmly against her clit. She cried out, but it was a good sound. One that made him feel about seven feet tall. He slid a finger inside her, felt the warm clamp of her insides, knew it would be incredible to slip inside that damp heat. But he also knew that it was too soon, that Pepper still needed to get used to the idea of them being together.

Because that was what Derek wanted. To be with Pepper.

Forget the movie. He'd find a way to do it on his own. Forget her family. He and Pepper could find a way to be happy together. Forget—

Her hands wound into his hair and yanked, hard enough to make his eyes water.

"Condom. Nightstand. Inside me. Now."

Goddamn she was sexy when she was bossy.

"Sweet—"

She growled. Literally growled and shoved him back, rolling to her side and scrabbling for the drawer. A second later, she held a foil square. A heartbeat after that it was open and she was rolling it down his length.

"I don't think—"

"Good. *Don't think.* Do." She finished putting on the condom then grabbed his hips, tugging him between her thighs. "Do *me.*"

How was he supposed to resist that?

Hands coming up to rest on either side of her head, he stared down into her eyes. Her pupils were dilated, the color almost completely obscured. A flush coated her cheeks. Her mouth was swollen from his kisses.

Her lips parted as he slid inside her and, fuck, she was tight. "God. I—"

He wanted to say he couldn't go slow, that he couldn't stop and wait for her to catch up, that he was on the edge.

But Pepper didn't give him the chance. She wrapped her legs tightly around his waist, pulled his head down to hers, and ground her hips to his.

And he was a goner.

Completely gone for Pepper.

He thrust in, slid out, matched the rhythm with his tongue. He balanced on one hand and hitched her knee higher with his other, needing to get deeper. His pulse pounded, sweat dripped down his spine, and his heart . . . well, that organ was torn wide open. So when Pepper gasped and tore her mouth free, lips forming an O as he hit just the right spot, he repeated the motion. And repeated it. And repeated it again. Over and over until his abs were burning, until he was more exhausted than after a long, hard workout.

Because it felt good for her, and he'd keep at it forever if she asked.

But she didn't need him to.

"Derek!" she cried out and then she was tightening around him, convulsing as she orgasmed, pulling him alongside her.

Pleasure exploded up his spine, through his limbs, sinking into his skin and soul alike. And when she finally quieted, he stilled his motions and rolled them to the side, feeling as though he'd been scoured from the inside out with steel wool.

He was tender. Vulnerable.

And it took just one look at Pepper's face to see she was feeling the same.

So he gathered her close, held her tight, and when she cried, he silently wiped her tears away.

———

DEREK HUNG up his cell with annoyance. Three calls to Peter O'Brien and three straight-to-voicemails in response.

The man was avoiding him.

But why?

He probably thought Derek was fed up with Pepper. And he was, he supposed, in a way. Fed up that Peter had manipulated him, and that his relationship with Pepper was tainted when Derek wanted it to be pure.

He wanted a movie style meet-cute, not his selfish need for self-fulfillment to be the start of him and Pepper.

Because there was only one thing that had made sense to him in the last few years, and that was spending time with Pepper.

A sparkle caught his focus.

"Wh—?"

Then he found he couldn't finish the question. He was mesmerized. By glass and wood, shells and jagged edges. He remembered the broken jar of shells, the piece of driftwood on her counter.

But this. *This* was so much more.

It was art. It was pain and heartbreak and being rebuilt stronger.

It was—

"Hey."

Pepper.

He turned and saw her propped against the doorframe of the kitchen, hair a mass of red tangles, bare thighs visible beneath the hem of his T-shirt she'd absconded.

"Hi." He crossed to her. "You okay?"

"Yup." A pause, eyes flicking ceiling-ward. "Hungry." She wrinkled her nose. "I think."

His lips twitched. "You sure?"

She nodded. "I really hope I didn't give you the plague."

He bent, kissed her neck. "Me, too. But I can't complain. That was . . ."

"A train wreck?"

"No." A nip on her throat for daring to discount herself. "Nothing about you is a train wreck. It was the best of my life. No lie," he added when she started to shake her head.

A swathe of pink danced across her cheekbones. "Really?"

"Really, *really*." He pressed his mouth to hers. "Now. Food."

# TWENTY-SIX

# A PLAGUE ON YOUR HOUSE, YOUR GOAT, YOUR COW

Pepper

DEREK'S LACK of fear of the plague didn't make him invulnerable to it. He succumbed just after dawn the next morning. Aside from guilt for contaminating the man, Pepper felt terrible that he was so miserable.

She was also glad to be past the projectile stage.

Really, *really* glad as she sat down to a bowl of pasta and a glass of wine. A soft knock at her door had her standing and staring longingly at the carb-filled deliciousness as she answered it.

Shannon stood on the threshold, looking perky and sweet as pie.

And really, it wasn't fair. In her past life, Pepper had stylists who didn't make her look nearly as good as her friend. But seriously, Shannon had the best clothes. Cute skirts, gorgeous blouses, and she was tall enough to not need heels. Or more likely, smart enough to not wear them while chasing kids around all day.

Today she wore a blue floral silk shirt. A matching bow on

the blouse tied near her neck, and she paired the whole look with black wide-legged trousers and sapphire flats.

Literally, the woman was surrounded by messy, germy, paint-covered, and snot-filled kids all day and she looked pristine.

And her husband was a total jerk for not appreciating it.

"Hey," Shannon said. "I came to see how you were faring."

"A little late," Pepper said with a smile. "Considering I've been recovered for over a day now."

"Well." A shrug. A smirk. "You had Derek with you."

"That I did." Pepper couldn't hold back her smile.

Shannon shrieked. "Oh, my God! You didn't! You *did*." She fist pumped and danced her way into the kitchen, snatching up the glass of wine from the table and taking a sip. "That's the best news I've had all day."

Pepper opened a cupboard and reached for another glass, filling it with more wine since Shannon had happily absconded with hers. She'd just lifted it to her mouth when Shannon asked, "Was he as good as he looks?"

And cue choking.

"I knew it!"

"I didn't say anything," she gasped out.

"You didn't have to." Shannon set the glass down then put her hands an obscene distance apart. "Now tell me. This long?" The space increased. "Or this?"

She rolled her eyes, grabbing a bowl and filling it with pasta, which she set in front of her friend. It wasn't wine and ice cream, but wine and carbs had to count for something, right? "You're terrible," she teased.

"True story," Shannon said, flashing a grin. "I also have a kindergartener at home and a husband who's not. I need to live vicariously through you."

"*Or*," Pepper said. "You have a really dirty mind and want me to make it worse."

"Not—" Shannon's expression went chagrined. "Fine. Okay. We both know that's true."

"That much I know," she agreed, snaking out a hand and grabbing her own bowl of pasta. "And not that you need to know, but yes he lived up to the hype," she said, not bothering to fight her smile this time. Then shook her head as Shannon squealed again, but she kept smiling all the same.

---

Sunlight streamed through the windows, a masculine arm sat heavy over her midsection.

Pepper turned her head carefully to the side, saw that Derek's eyes were closed and his breathing was even. That was the only reason why she did it.

Because he was asleep.

She pressed her nose to his neck and inhaled.

Good God, it was better than chocolate.

Blasphemy, she knew. But still the truth.

"Did you just sniff me?"

Her eyes flew open and all breath halted in her lungs. No, she would absolutely not admit that she'd been sniffing Derek. "No. I was breathing," she said. "I think you know it, seeing as it's a critical bodily function."

"Hmm." His eyes were open and blazed with a look that set her nerves on high alert.

"How are you feeling?" she asked.

He still looked pale, but had survived the requisite forty-eight hours.

"Better," he said then wrinkled his nose. "But I need dousing in bleach. I stink."

"You smell incredible."

Dimple alert. "*Ah*. But I thought you said you weren't sniffing me."

"I wasn't." She glared, twisting the sheet in her fingers. "But I *can* smell you know. And no, you don't smell bad."

"Mmmhmm." Derek gently pried her fingers free of the sheet. "Likely"—he ripped the cotton off her body—"story."

"What—?"

She didn't get the chance to finish the question because Derek was suddenly between her thighs, nose pressed against her pussy, inhaling deeply. Hot breath permeated the lace underwear she wore when he spoke. "*I'm* sniffing *you*."

Creepy.

As in his words should have been. But coming from Derek, his voice all gravelly, his face nuzzling into her . . . yeah, not so much creepy as the hottest thing she'd ever experienced. Moisture pooled between her legs, soaking her panties, filling the air with a different scent altogether.

Female arousal.

It should have embarrassed her. It didn't.

Derek tugged the hem of her underwear to one side and traced his tongue up. Then back down.

She shuddered, hands coming up to clench at his hair.

"Like that, baby?" he asked.

"You know I do," she said. "But shouldn't you be—" Her words faltered because he'd done that thing again with his tongue. The twist-flick against her clit that made her stupid.

She'd once thought his dimples his most dangerous body part.

She'd been wrong. That particular award went to his tongue.

It gave her sweet words, hopeful sentiments, and was the complete and totalitarian ruler of her lady business. Another flick had all rational—and *irrational*, it had to be said—thoughts fleeing her mind. Sensation took over everything. The heat building within her center, flooding her legs and torso, pleasure twisting her higher and higher and higher until—

She screamed his name and exploded.

"I *was* smelling you," Pepper murmured, when the power of speech eventually returned to her.

Derek laughed. "I know." He pushed up and gathered her in his arms, sniffing deeply in her neck. "And I don't care."

## TWENTY-SEVEN
## SPICING THINGS UP

THE LAST TWO weeks had been the happiest of Pepper's life.

Derek was busy most of the days, taking his camera and disappearing from her bed and into the mysterious streets of Stoneybrook—okay, not so much. But while she didn't understand the appeal of documenting every single piece of typical small town America as he did, she had seen some footage.

It was amazing.

He seemed to find the unique beauty in even the simplest parts of Stoneybrook. A portion of peeling paint framed by blooming flowers, the Bert's Burgers sign overwhelmed by the ocean in the background.

And that was just the town itself. When he captured the people within, the heart and blood of Stoneybrook, something even more magical occurred.

Freckles across a pale nose, a toothy smile, ice-cream-coated lips. Wrinkles at the corners of eyes, wispy white hair. Young and old. Naïve and jaded. He had an innate ability to capture the hidden magnificence within, to celebrate what made each person and object unique.

He was brilliant, and she understood why her father had joined the venture.

Documentaries weren't O'Brien Films' cash cow, but Peter loved discovering new talent. It was clear Derek was exactly that.

"Have you filmed any other towns?" she asked.

They were sprawled across her bed, his laptop between them as he showed her the footage from that day.

He closed the window on the screen then opened another. "Yes. But only a little. I was supposed to leave to scout the new location a couple weeks ago."

Pepper stilled. "You mean before my father ordered you to babysit me."

He shrugged. "I needed to shoot here, too—"

"Except you *hadn't* planned to." She straightened, irritation coursing through her.

Their time together had been so blissful that she'd been able to forget the cause.

Her father.

He'd orchestrated the entire thing, was probably sitting back, rubbing his hands together and saying, "Excellent" like George Burns from *The Simpsons*.

"You should go." She shoved his shoulder.

Derek glanced up, brows drawn tight. "Now?"

Pepper's eyes flicked to the windows. It was dark outside, the sound of waves crashing along the shore trickling into the cottage. "No. Tomorrow," she said. "Start shooting the new town."

"I'm shooting *here*." He closed the laptop and set it on the floor. "What's really going on?"

"You're here because of my father." She sighed, gut twisting. She always messed up everything. "I'm not going to let him meddle with your dreams."

"My dream has waited for twenty-years," he said. "It can wait until after your brother's wedding." When she opened her mouth to protest, he continued, "And anyway, I'm going to have to come back with the crew. The footage is barely passable as test shots. The professionals need to come in and take over."

Her lips tightened. "What you've filmed is incredible."

"Passable." He bent and kissed her. "Barely. Aside from that, we're leaving for your brother's wedding in just under a week. Why should I go now? I'd have to fly back before we flew down together."

The man had a point. Unfortunately.

"We could fly separately."

"Pepper." He said her name in a tone that made a shiver roll down her spine. All growly and ridiculous, and yet her body still liked it. "What is this really about?"

"What's *what* about?"

Derek just stared at her.

She wouldn't cave. She wouldn't cave. She wouldn't—

Argh. "Fine. I'm having a moment of what-in-the-hell-are-we-doing, okay? You and I don't make any sense. I'm a mess. I don't have a job—"

"Neither do I."

She threw a frustrated hand out. "Except you're filming a movie."

He captured it, brought her palm to his lips. "And you're making sculptures."

Her breath caught. She *had* been sculpting. But she'd been careful to not mention it, afraid . . . well, she wasn't exactly sure what she was afraid of. Judgment? Derision? She couldn't draw worth a damn, couldn't sew a straight line, couldn't—

How could she expect to make art?

"They're amazing," he said softly, rolling toward her and tucking a strand of hair behind her ear. "As unique as you are."

The word *unique* made her stiffen and pull back.

Unique. Unique. Pepper was *unique*—usually said with derision.

Uniquely klutzy. Uniquely different. Uniquely disastrous and—

*Fuck that.*

She was so damned tired of beating herself up, and yet the words, engrained so deeply after so many years, slipped from her anyway. "You're too good for me, Derek."

"Bullshit," he snapped.

Her eyes flew up.

"I'm going to say something that might piss you off," he said as he sat up and thrust a hand through his hair. "Hell, I *hope* it pisses you off. I want you to fight for once. For yourself. For us. For something that you want. Who gives a fuck if you're not Hollywood? Fuck Hollywood. Fuck your parents for treating you like shit. Fuck me for making you face this. Pepper"—he forced a breath, softened his voice—"*baby*, you deserve good things. But you need to go after those good things. Otherwise, you'll always be here."

"I—"

"And I don't mean here in Stoneybrook," he said. "I mean here in your head, constantly degrading yourself, thinking you're not worth it." He stroked a finger down her cheek. "You deserve more than just existing. You deserve to be happy." His chest was heaving, eyes filled with an intensity that made the air freeze in her lungs.

He was right.

The destructive part of her would have loved to deny him that, but the simple truth was he was correct. She should fight for all of those things.

She just wasn't sure she had the courage to.

If she wasn't a train wreck then what was she?

Sometimes it was easier being the constant screw up, not having anyone expect things of her. Because when she failed . . . well, that was because she never had a chance to succeed in the first place.

But if she really wanted to succeed then she had to put that particular security blanket aside.

Courage. She needed to find it.

"I'm happy when I'm with you," she said quietly.

All of the tension drained from Derek's body. "Me too."

"Good." A beat. "But I'm not sure I have the strength to fight for it."

His face softened. "You do, sweetheart." He touched her chest, right above her heart. "It's in here already."

Hope filled her. Maybe she could do this. Maybe she could fight for it.

"Derek."

"No arguments with the man who bought you cheesecake."

She grinned. He had bought her cheesecake. Of the full-fat variety. Also . . . God, she loved the man.

It was too early to say such craziness, of course.

But maybe she could show him.

Maybe through loving him, she could find the strength to love herself.

Rolling away from him, she reached for a bottle in her nightstand. Shannon had given it to her as a joke, but really, what man wouldn't like a blowy? Mentally, she stopped and shook her head at herself. Grown women did not say *blowy*. They were confident in their sexual prowess—

Ugh. They didn't say *prowess* either.

It was desire and fellatio, fucking and blow jobs. Come on now.

She opened the bottle.

"You okay over there?" Derek's voice was confused.

"Yup." She started a quick scan of the label, but then the bed shifted, Derek starting to lean over to see what she was doing.

Crap. Rapidly, she spritzed the bottle in her mouth three or four or . . . ten times. The spray was supposed to relax her throat muscles enough to take him a little deeper than normal.

If she combined the amount of occasions he'd gone down on her during the last two weeks with his speech from earlier then he really deserved something special.

"Pepper?"

"Shh," she told him, though her words felt odd. The spray must already be working. Which was a good thing. The gag reflex was strong with this one . . . or, she mentally shook her head, with *her*.

Forcing her mind to stop, she tore off her T-shirt.

"Okay, I'm liking this," Derek said, leaning back onto the pillows with a grin.

"You'll—" She stopped because the word was slurred. Okay, deep throat gel meant no talking.

Which was fine.

She didn't need talking. She needed his pants off.

## TWENTY-EIGHT

# NUMB IS GOOD, RIGHT?

Derek

DEREK WAS HAVING the time of his life . . . until he wasn't.

Pleasure coursed through his body as he enjoyed the slide of Pepper's incredible mouth up and down, deeper than he would have thought possible.

It began with a tingle. A slight numbing sensation. At first he didn't recognize it, not until it spread farther.

"Uh."

"Mmm," Pepper said, handing working up and down. He thought he felt it, he *could* almost feel it, though it was almost phantom-limb-like.

He wanted to feel it.

But he didn't.

"Pepper." He put his hands on her shoulders, tugging her back. "Something's wrong."

Her head tilted up. "Shmerf's smong?"

He blinked. "What?"

"Eh shaid shwats shrong?"

She stopped, released her grip on his erection—which was

still going strong despite the numbness—and placed a hand to her mouth.

"Sweetheart." He pushed up, pressed a gentle finger to her lips. "Is your mouth numb too?"

A nod, eyes wide.

Then she flopped back onto the mattress with a groan.

"What is it?"

Her hand slid out to the side, pointing at her nightstand.

With a frown, Derek leaned over her. Nothing was there. He pulled open the drawer and saw a little green bottle on top of a book.

"DeepEaze?" he murmured and picked up the palm-sized container.

Another groan, followed by the *thwack* of a pillow covering a face.

He squinted, studying the label with a growing mix of horror and amusement. "Spray one time on the back of the throat," he read aloud, "to relax muscles and bring extra pleasure for your partner."

"Shone shime?" came Pepper's muffled voice.

Derek was somehow starting to translate her slurred speech. "One time," he repeated. "How many sprays did you do?"

"Shten."

"*Ten?*" He glanced down at his cock. It was thrusting forward, still hard despite the lack of feeling.

She moaned. He grinned. He couldn't help it.

"God I love you, Pepper O'Brien."

"Shwat?" She popped up like a whack-a-mole.

He pressed a kiss to her lips, not sure if she could feel it, but unable to stop himself from doing so anyway.

"It's supposed to wear off in fifteen minutes," he murmured, running a hand up her bare thigh. She was still naked. He flicked his fingers between her legs. Wet. Still wet. "What should we do to pass the time?"

Her breath caught.

Derek bent, nuzzling between her breasts, coaxing her to lean back against the mattress.

"Sh—"

"Hush." He slipped down and proceeded to kiss her just the way she liked it.

Just the way *he* liked it.

---

DEREK DIALED Peter O'Brien's number for the tenth time that week, listening to the *ring-ring, ring-ring.*

It went to voicemail.

Again.

He cursed, the stress of the unfinished business with Pepper's father screwing with his head. He needed to end things before they got even more complicated. But that was tough to do when the man was avoiding him.

And there was absolutely no doubt about that.

The only thing that Derek was questioning was why.

Probably, the man thought he wanted to skip out on his baby-sitting duties. In reality, he wanted to skip out on film-making duties.

All his life, he'd wanted to be different from his family. Wanted to stand out from the Cashette name, do something more valuable than vetting celebrity contracts and squeezing every dollar out of a settlement.

He'd tried family law. Total fail. Divorce proceedings were even more heartbreaking than Hollywood eccentricities. Kids in the middle, fighting over the dog, the house, the car . . . the books.

Seriously. He'd once represented a woman who was suing her ex-husband for their collection of books.

Which perhaps would have been understandable if they'd been first editions or even heirlooms.

But they hadn't been.

Instead, the woman had sued for dog-eared paperbacks, worn hardcovers.

Of course, now that he was removed from his old life, he thought he understood why she'd battled so hard. They weren't just books. They weren't objects that were valuable, or not *necessarily* valuable anyway.

Memories created their value. The way they'd been so carefully loved over the years. Held close, read, and reread. Appreciated. Enjoyed.

That was why the books were important.

They had worth.

And he was looking for *his* worth.

Derek had thought it might come in the form of the documentary, but that dream seemed so small and unimportant now.

Pepper was more than financing. She was a whirlwind, yes, but one of kindness and deep throat gel, of strength to strike out on her own and involuntary numbness. She was different.

Which was a good thing.

It made him want to be different, too.

Maybe he would need to go back to practicing law, save more money before he was able to film his movie.

But in doing that he could keep his soul, not having traded it for easy money and a quick shot at a dream.

He would earn his dream.

On his own.

Derek paused, phone in hand, staring out the dark window above Pepper's kitchen sink. Only a few days remained before the wedding and it's various pre and post events.

Paul's impending marriage felt like both a beginning and an end. He would finally be able to tell Peter that the deal was off and damn the consequences.

Then he could win the girl.

Forever.

# TWENTY-NINE

# WEDDING BELLS

Pepper

PEPPER STARED at the doorway of the private jet as though it were the entrance to the gallows.

"Come on," Derek said. "It's not as bad as that."

She remembered the last time she'd seen Andy, balls deep in his assistant, and shuddered. It was why she'd left for Stoneybrook. The final straw after her reckless endangerment of Hollywood—studio spaces and stars alike.

"It's pretty bad," she muttered, carefully climbing the set of metal steps leading up into the plane. They were covered in a red carpet (because of course they were) that appeared decidedly out of place in the regional airport outside of town. Then again, everything seemed out of place in the quaint city, an assault on the slice of sanctuary she'd created for herself.

A slice that now included Derek.

Swallowing hard, Pepper stepped through the doorway. Plush cream leather, tan carpet, a fleet of stewardesses awaiting her every whim.

"We'll be on our way in a jiffy, Ms. O'Brien," the pilot said cheerily. He was young, perhaps even younger than her, and sexy—usage of the word *jiffy* aside. Tall, tan, bright white teeth. No scruff, she thought, tilting her head slightly as he turned away.

Some scruff on that chin would have definitely been the cherry on top.

Her head tilted to the side as he walked away. Or maybe that cherry was his a—

Derek grunted and slid by her, shooting a dark look toward the captain. "He said *jiffy*."

Pepper's lips twitched. "So he did, but that doesn't mean he's not pretty to look at."

"And they say men are pigs."

"What would that make me? A sow?"

He snorted, but his eyes were amused. "I'm not touching that one."

She laughed and closed the distance between them. "I happen to like it when you touch *me*."

Amusement went by the wayside. The heat in his gaze seared right through her. "I know."

Eek.

She pulled at the collar of her shirt, her temperature skyrocketing because when Derek got all deep and dark and growly, her insides turned straight into mush.

"Mimosa?" the stewardess asked.

Pepper didn't know this one's name. In fact, she didn't know any of their names. Which was a jerk move on her part she supposed, but turnover of O'Brien flight attendants tended to be high.

Most thought it was the ticket to the big leagues, and when it proved not to be the easy road to a starring role in a blockbuster . . .

Yeah. They didn't hang around long.

She accepted the glass and thanked the beautiful, blond, bouncy woman genuinely. Most of that genuineness came from Derek not paying her the least bit of masculine attention. *She'd* ogled the pilot nearly into submission and now was happy that Derek had ignored the buxom flight attendant.

Double standards existed and in this case, she couldn't find the proper amount of outrage.

Pepper was just happy that Derek only seemed to have eyes for her.

Of course, Andy had once been that way too.

*No.* She pushed that cruel little voice out of her mind, buckled her seatbelt, and held on.

She wasn't going to poison this time with Derek with doubts just because she was on edge. Attending an event that should have been her wedding and had to play nice with her cheating, ex-fiancé didn't matter because she and Andy were done.

*Way* done.

And now she was with Derek.

He was different. They were different together. *She* was different with him.

Until he wasn't.

Until they weren't.

Until *she* wasn't.

PEPPER DIDN'T RECOGNIZE the slight change in tenor between her and Derek at first.

Initially, it was chaos with the landing and deplaning, going through customs and locating their car, then checking into the hotel. If Derek didn't hold her hand in the lobby it was because they were both carrying too many things. If he seemed sharp with her when she asked why he'd gotten his own room, it was because he was tired.

If he dropped her at her door with the barest peck on the cheek it was because her mother was waiting impatiently in the hall and *needed* her immediately. Derek was being considerate by taking care of her bags.

"It's all terrible," her mother hissed, yanking her down the hall and away from him. "That cow—"

Pepper gasped. Even if Summer was having a bridezilla moment, it wasn't fair to refer to her as a cow. Weddings were stressful. "Mom! Summer isn't—"

"No," Poppy snapped. "That *woman* is a control freak."

"*What* woman?"

"Her. *Mother.*"

The two words may as well have been a curse for as violently as Poppy spat them. They also should not have made Pepper's lips twitch.

She glanced back over her shoulder at Derek.

He stood outside their rooms and was glaring down at his phone, typing furiously. But as though he felt her eyes on him, he glanced up.

She mouthed, "Are you okay?"

He nodded, but his smile was off.

Not that she had the chance to investigate it since Poppy was towing her down the hallway. They burst through a door and into a room filled with . . . more chaos.

Summer was crying. A makeup artist was armed with a tissue in one hand and a tube of concealer in the other. A pink dress was draped on a hanger, marred with a huge red smear of something—

Pepper's eyes flew heavenward. *Please not blood. Please not blood.*

One of the bridesmaids—or a woman she presumed was a

bridesmaid, since she'd never met any of the bridal party except Andy and Derek—was on her phone, her face pale, her tone panicked.

"Why would you do that?" Summer shrieked at her. "Ketchup in a bridal suite! *Ketchup!*"

Well, at least it wasn't blood.

Poppy left Pepper, crossing to Summer and was nearly elbowed out of the way when Summer's mother shoved herself between them. A terse discussion ensued as both accused the other of upsetting Summer the most.

Pepper sighed and walked across the room, plucking the dress from where it was hung on the back of a door then left the suite and headed for the front desk.

"Kitchen?" she asked.

"Uh—w-why?" the college kid behind it stammered out.

Pepper knew she looked strange, carrying a neon pink dress —that must be clashing horribly with her bright ass hair—and asking for directions to a place where guests didn't normally go, but she did not have time for this.

So she channeled her inner Peter O'Brien and fixed him with a glare that would send lesser minions running. "Tell me where the kitchens are."

He caved. She smiled. Maid of honor duties, yup, she was rocking them.

Unfortunately, when she spun around she realized the little man-child hadn't actually caved because of her glare and tone.

He'd crumpled because her father was behind her, arms crossed, brows pulled down imperiously, the groomsmen— including Andy, Derek, and Paul—gathered behind him.

"Baby girl," he father boomed, leaning close to give her air kisses. Never real hugs. Nor kisses. Always air. Always for show. "Derek here tells me you were no trouble on the plane, but"—he laughed, glanced down at the stained dress in her hands—"I see that disaster didn't stay away for long."

He turned and thumped Derek's shoulder. "Told you she needs a keeper."

Derek's eyes were icy cold. "I don't—"

"Want to be her keeper?" Andy chimed in. His cruel laughter slithered down Pepper's spine and she shivered. "Join the crowd, bro."

She rolled her eyes and started to walk away, but Paul caught her arm.

"I knew you'd ruin something," he hissed. "That's Summer's—"

"Pepper just got here," Derek said. "She couldn't have—"

"Trust me," Paul said. "She *could*."

"Hey. Just ignore him," Pepper said, turning her back on her brother and lightly touching Derek's chest. "I—"

He jumped back, as though her touch was a rattlesnake bite.

The slice of pain across her heart might as well have been one.

Derek thrust a hand through his hair, glanced over her shoulder. "Peter, could I have a moment?"

"Derek," she began.

"Not now," he said.

"I—"

"*Later*," he snapped. He. Snapped. At. *Her*.

Andy laughed. "Need a firm hand with our Pep here." He turned to Paul. "Come on. Let's hit the bar. I need something to drink in order to deal with *everything*." His stare was heavy and frosty and wholly on Pepper, telling her all she needed to know about dealing with *everything*.

*Everything* being her.

Even though he was the asshole who cheated.

"*Pep*," Derek said, eyes cool as they fixed her in place,

"needs a lot of things. The least of which is going to take care of that dress."

*What the fuck?*

Her breath hitched, eyes burning. Using that nickname. The dismissal in his words. How cold his gaze was as he stared at her. What the hell had happened for him to pull such a Jekyll and Hyde?

Paul and Andy laughed before turning and heading out of the lobby, presumably to find that bar.

Derek was shoulder to shoulder with her father by the time she recovered from the frosty words, his phone out again as he scrolled through some document on the screen. He said something to Peter, but just as her father began to respond, his assistant came up to the pair, and Derek was pushed out of the conversation. His jaw tightened, his hand burrowed through his hair again, and as the conversation between her father and his assistant continued, Derek's shoulders slumped. His phone went back into his pocket, and he crossed over to her.

"I'll see you at the party," he said, fingers brushing the back of her hand as he walked away.

Pepper stood there for a moment as he disappeared, shocked and hurt and confused. She wanted to go after him, because Derek was obviously upset by something, but this wasn't the place to hash it out.

They could do that . . . she sighed, pushed the sting of his words away, later.

AND IF BY *later* she meant, after she'd managed to baking-soda-out the stain and use a blow dryer to dry the dress, or when she waited for him to escort her to the coed bridal shower that she was now late for—

*Hell.* She didn't know what any of it meant. The flight had been uneventful, quiet, as they'd read their respective books. She hadn't done *anything* and—

Fuck. Stop. She hated her first thought was that she was to blame.

If he had a problem then he could just bring it up and discuss it with her like a rational human being. Otherwise, she was as tired of being a punching bag as she was tired of waiting for his sexy ass to meet her for the shower.

Time to go.

Chin up. Shoulders back. Her bag was on the table by the sliding glass doors leading out to the ocean. A floor-to-ceiling view of the setting sun, pale white sand turned shades of pink and red and orange, turquoise waves tipped in white.

It was paradise.

And . . . it still broke her heart. Just the slightly damaged portion, cracking off the corner, making old wounds ache all over again.

Because Andy had been different, too.

Or she'd thought so, anyway.

Their wedding was supposed to have been a new start for her, and while she was relieved she'd discovered what a snake he was before their vows and content that her future had taken a new turn, presumably with Derek—though given their last inter-action she was now unsure of what had seemed so certain on the mainland—she couldn't help but feel as though things hadn't really changed.

She was still a mess. Still fumbling her way through life. She didn't have a purpose, a direction, a—

*Enough.*

Her breath caught as Derek left his suite, next door to hers, and headed down the beach to a white tent filled with tables and flowers, lit with torches and twinkly lights.

He didn't glance back.

Not once.

Her heart shattered a little more.

Because she was starting to think that Derek *wasn't* different, after all. That what they had *wasn't* actually special. That while she'd been seeing, *feeling* something between them, there wasn't anything at all that truly connected them.

Or nothing more than her father and his wishes, and Derek's yearning to finish his film.

Which really sucked.

But what could she do? She couldn't make Derek love her. She couldn't change her father. She could only live her life and just stop, *stop* being a fucking punching bag. So, even though her heart was crumbling, Pepper lifted her chin, straightened her spine.

Maybe she *had* made a mistake. Maybe Derek really was a jerk who'd used her.

But she wouldn't let him break her.

Life went on. She could heal her hurts, dry her tears.

Could put them aside and just get through this week, see her brother get married.

Then she could move on and not look back.

Ever.

She picked up her purse and walked out the door.

The sand was cold beneath her bare toes.

Just like her heart.

# THIRTY
## IT WOULD BE FUN, THEY SAID

PEPPER TOOK her time reaching the tent. She wasn't acting the coward, or not entirely anyway. The slow steps allowed her a moment to breathe, to shore up those empty holes inside her.

Laughter trickled across the sand, blurring with the crash of the waves.

It was a soothing sort of sound, the laughter mingling with the ocean, but its peaceful nature was also entirely deceptive of what awaited her inside.

Barbed comments, disdain. Andy as the best man.

He was the shark on shore, one who would certainly take a limb given half a chance. He'd always liked to "tease" her about her ineptitudes, laugh at her ill-grace, and she hated that being here was a reminder that she'd been weak enough to take his cruelty for so long.

*Oh Pep, what would we do if we didn't have you to laugh at?*

*Hit another Oscar-winner, Pep? Your father needs the tax deduction.*

Ugh. She'd been weak and cowed and pathetic. Still, the good thing about being a grown-up was that she could be self-aware, could change. She wasn't the same person anymore, and there was no way she'd allow herself to be harassed.

So, bring it, Andy the Asshole.

The thing about taking slow, small steps was that even though she wasn't in a hurry to join the festivities, those steps meant she was still moving forward. Which meant that she eventually made it to the shower, to the people inside.

The inside of the white canvas tent was as gorgeous as the view from the outside and exactly as she'd pictured it when she'd ordered the decorations nearly a year before. Round tables lushly covered in floral arrangements, hundreds of candles scattered throughout. Crisp linens and glittering flatware.

A band was set up behind a dance floor occupying one corner of the covering, large round tables filled the rest of the space.

The wait staff wore precisely ironed white shirts and pink ties. It was the same shade as the flowers, as the dress hanging in Pepper's suite, and the single thing Summer had changed. Pepper loved the ocean and all its blues. Summer, on the other hand, preferred pink. Well, preferred wasn't the right word. The bride was obsessed with it, and her wedding would be an explosion of it.

A marginally tasteful, but very expensive explosion.

Pepto-Bismol all the same.

"Pepper!" The harsh squeal rent the air and told her several things all at once.

One. Summer was drinking.

Two. A lot.

Three. She was drinking because things weren't going well.

And time for Pepper's maid of honor duties.

With a sigh, she plastered on a smile and hurried over to Summer.

"I'm so happy for you!" They hugged, and the stench of

tequila hit her in the face. Good God, did it *always* have to be tequila? Their college days were over, and the sheer number of tequila-induced hangovers they'd experienced together should have turned Summer—as it had Pepper—off the stuff forever.

Apparently, the bride didn't have the same qualms that she did.

Or, perhaps more likely, Summer was desperate.

It took two point two seconds to figure out why her friend was drinking battery acid.

Mother.

Rather, *mothers*.

As in the two plastic-surgery-enhanced, looked-thirty-five-but-were-actually-fifty blond (and only blond, because all those gray hairs had been dyed into submission), plucked, tightened, *tucked* mothers were glaring angrily at one another.

"What happened?" she murmured softly to Summer.

Apparently not softly enough because Summer's mom—who was unfortunately named Candy—pointed one pink-painted fingernail at Pepper's mom and shrieked, "Poppy said I'm fat."

Oh boy.

If there was something in their circle even more unforgive-able than insulting someone behind their back, it was insulting someone to their front.

Paul kissed Summer on the cheek. "The boys and I are off then." He sped out of the tent, pathetic pansy that he was, with the rest of the men, including—glarey eyes—Andy, on their heels. Derek followed as well, but paused, sending her a look that was both distant and unreadable before heading out onto the beach.

Cowards. The lot of them.

"I didn't—" Poppy began.

"You most certainly—" Candy interrupted.

"Where's the wedding planner?" Pepper asked Summer. She knew the resort provided one.

"Sick," Summer wailed. "They sent her assistant, but my mother yelled at her and she left and—"

Candy bristled. "I *did not*—"

"Oh yes, you did."

Voices rose, fingers pointed, cheeks heated and—

Pepper didn't think, she reacted.

She gripped the arm of the girl next to her and ordered, "Go into that room"—she indicated the nearest suite—"and grab as many rolls of toilet paper as you can."

When the girl didn't move, only turned and stared at Pepper down her perfectly sculpted nose, Pepper gave her a shove. "Now!" she growled.

The girl paled and took off.

"You." She pointed at the nearest waiter. "Get a bag. Any bag and fill it with random things."

"Ran—"

Pepper interrupted the question. "Like gum and a comb, a fork, lipstick, random everyday objects. About ten of them, put them in a bag, and bring it to me. Now!"

The next waiter was dispatched for pens and paper.

When they'd gone, she turned toward the quibbling mothers and girded her loins.

"Games!" She shouted over the din, grabbing Summer's arm and tugging her toward the dance floor. "It's time for games!"

The crowd, which had been tennis-match-style spectating, or more plainly, had been swiveling glances between the two women turned to face her.

Pepper gulped, but she wasn't a coward, dammit. Plus, she'd seen this online and had always wanted to play it. Her shower had been too posh for games, so she might as well take some enjoyment in this train wreck of a gathering.

"Come on! Come on!" The women slowly made their way to the dance floor. "Now we need to break up into teams of three. Where's—Oh! Good," she said when the girl she'd sent off for toilet paper returned, arms laden.

"What are you doing?"

Shivers down her spine. Derek's voice *always* gave her shivers. She supposed it always would, even when he was hissing angrily at her.

"I'm fixing this," she snapped back. The ire in her tone made her proud. He was the one acting like an ass. Hot, cold, distant, not.

"With toilet paper?" he asked sarcastically.

"Yes." She turned her back on him and counted, "One, two, three." Sectioning off a group while being careful to separate Poppy and Candy.

"Pepper—" He grabbed her arm.

She ripped it free. "Stop pretending to care, Derek." Her finger jabbed into his chest. "You got me here safe and sound. Your job is done. Now leave me alone."

Derek's mouth fell open, but Pepper was done.

He didn't want to be with her, fine. He *did* want to be with her, then great. Stop treating her like crap and she'd think about whether or not she wanted to forgive him. But in the meantime, she wanted him to stop, to go away, to not continue ingraining himself deeper within her, making her care, making her feel—

She turned her back on him.

"Pepper," Derek said softly.

Hope filled her. Maybe . . .

"Am I reading this wrong?" she asked, rotating around because she owed it to herself to make this crystal clear with Derek, to not run just because things weren't perfectly smooth and happy. More grown-up behavior. More being strong and brave."Am I overreacting or going crazy because this was supposed to be my wedding? Am I seeing this correctly?" She reached for his hand, but he backed up a step, an action that had her trying not to flinch. "Did you change your mind? Or d-do you want to be with me? Out in the open so everyone knows we're together?"

Silence.

Then two words that iced over her blood. "I can't."

Pepper forced a smile, and it felt grotesque on her face. "That's what I thought." A beat. "Thanks for making things clear."

"I—"

This time when she turned away, she stayed that way, even though the space between her shoulder blades burned.

Eventually, Derek left, and took all of her hope, her desires that she'd just been imaging things right along with him.

Chin up.

She could deal with her hurt later.

For now she had a shower to save.

For no other reason than she wasn't going to let this wedding go down without a fight. It might not be hers any longer, but it was going to be a success, dammit. And because . . . even though she and Summer had grown apart, their lives deviating and changing, once upon a time, Summer had been her friend. A good one.

And her friend deserved something fun and nice and as drama-free as possible.

Even if it had once been Pepper's.

Even if she was marrying Paul.

Even if she was going to cut ties with everyone after this.

Pepper could still stave off disaster and do this one nice thing.

"Two rolls per team," she instructed the girl who'd brought the toilet paper then pulled out her phone and brought up her stopwatch feature, announcing once everyone had their respective materials, "You have five minutes to make one wedding dress. Pick your model. The other two are the designers. Any style you want and agree on, but the only material you can use is toilet paper. Okay?"

The women looked at her as though she'd grown two extra heads.

This would require a little coaxing . . . or perhaps, a little healthy competition.

"Winning team gets bragging rights and drinks on me!" She readied her finger over the start button on the timer and said, "Three. Two. One. Go!" She tapped her screen.

That "Go!" was enough to get the women moving.

Or maybe it was the free booze and bragging rights.

But those ladies could move. Purses hit the ground, toilet paper rolls were ripped open, and "models" were selected.

Pepper stayed out of the mix, snapping some pictures as the women worked, but mostly just watching the timer and keeping her brand of disaster far, far away from drinking women on heels and glassware. One of the servers she'd sent returned to her side, a bag in hand. She checked the objects inside, just to be sure he hadn't stuck a knife or Great White Shark inside—because really, her luck—and thanked him.

No weapons.

Just Chapstick, a comb, a toothbrush—hopefully unused, but she wasn't going to quibble at this point—

"Two minutes!" she called to the women.

A fork, a drink umbrella, a seashell, and a quarter rounded out the items. Seven wasn't ten, but it would do on short notice.

She set the bag on a table and started dragging chairs over. The wait staff caught on quickly and helped her make a circle.

"Thirty seconds!"

A trill of voices greeted her in response—laughter and

dismay and cheers all mixed together. This was actually working. They were actually having fun.

And the dresses were pretty good. Especially Summer's. Her teammates had managed to make a large bow out of the paper, tucking it hilariously above her derriere and creating a large train out of strips from the rolls.

It wasn't the neatest construction but the most creative.

And also Pepper figured that Summer was the one most likely to need more alcohol.

While the bartender was making the winning team their drinks, she herded Summer and company to the chairs.

"Sit," she ordered, holding the sack, paper, and pens. "Next game, everyone!"

As she explained the rules—basically trying to figure out the objects within the bag without peeking inside—she glanced up and saw Derek hadn't really left.

Or not completely anyway.

He was skulking in the shadows outside the dance floor, staring at her with something akin to wonderment. Because she'd managed to play a few games without setting fire to the tent? Because she hadn't broken any ankles—hers or otherwise?

Or because she'd stepped up when Summer had needed her?

Deliberately, she turned her back and called over her trusty waiter friend. His name was Clark, she'd discovered, and he was happy to go along with whatever Pepper came up with so as not to have a tent full of angry women.

"So what exactly happened to the wedding planner?" she asked.

"Stomach flu," he said.

Pepper shuddered, still too close to her own bout of the stuff to not empathize.

"Can you send appetizers out?" she asked. "Then help me

bring the gifts over?" she asked. "*Then* make sure dinner is ready to serve?"

He nodded. "Food. Gifts. Food."

One half of her mouth turned up. "Food to soak up the booze. Gifts to distract. More food to calm the beasts."

Clark smiled. "Makes sense."

Pepper began making trips with the presents, setting them behind Summer's chair as the bag made its way around the circle.

"I can't figure out the last one—"

"How many did you feel?"

"*Seven?* I only got six."

"But what about the other—"

By the time the gifts were over to Summer, the bag had made it's circle and Pepper revealed the objects.

There were groans as she did so, but they were good-natured, and mixed with laughter. The last made her relax because both moms—seated on opposite sides of the circle—were laughing again. Appetizers were served, a winner was chosen, and gifts were opened as Pepper dutifully recorded their contents and giver.

Only when the group had sat down to their respective tables and were eating, soft music playing in the background, did the men reappear.

Derek wasn't with them.

Not that it mattered.

Because Andy *was*.

And that mattered. Unfortunately.

Either way, it had already been a long week and they were T-minus five hours into wedding festivities.

She couldn't wait for tomorrow.

Joy.

# THIRTY-ONE

# I WILL FIND YOU AND I WILL KILL YOU

SLIPPING out of the tent seemed the wisest course of action. Emotions were back under control. Food was tempering the booze in Summer's stomach. Pepper was no longer needed.

She'd barely escaped the glow of the tent's torches before his voice reached hers.

"Pep in your step!"

Great. *He* was drunk, too.

She stopped and turned to face Andy, who was weaving his way toward her.

"Pepper," he slurred. "How are you, baby?" He slung a heavy arm around her shoulders, nearly toppling her to the ground.

Thank God she was barefoot. Heels and she would have ended up on her ass.

"I'm not your baby," she said, slipping from beneath his arm and turning away.

"Pep, baby, it was one girl, one time."

"It was at least five girls and more times than I want to know." A slow rotation, one of her brows rising. "Plus, last I heard you were engaged to that *one time*. What happened? She dump you for someone with more clout?"

"You're such a bitch," Andy snapped, proving that once again, he could pivot as quickly on his emotions—from loving to mean as a snake, from caring to fucking any other woman in sight. "Always have been. So fucking cold in bed that my cock about froze off. *Of course* I had to find someone else."

Andy the Asshole had made his reappearance.

The only good thing was finding out that his words didn't have the power to wound her. Not any longer.

Finally, something good she'd discovered this weekend.

"Nice, Andy." She rolled her eyes. "Always so classy."

She whirled away before turning back.

He wouldn't listen, but she might as well get this off her chest. It was like puking—one always felt better after the deed was done, not worse. This would be a cathartic release for her, even though he wouldn't care.

She jabbed a finger into his chest. "I tried to be perfect for you and ended up losing myself. And for what? So you'd love me more? So you'd be faithful to me?" She threw up both hands. "It was all for nothing. At the end of the day, I wasn't happy with myself and, God knows, I couldn't make you happy."

"I'm—"

"And if we're listing off reasons for why our relationship would have never worked, I've got my own set."

"You—"

She ticked them off one by one. "First, you don't like dogs. Second, you prefer soggy bacon. What kind of monster doesn't like crispy bacon?" She took a breath. This man had very nearly broken her. The cheating. The insults. The never-measuring-up. Their relationship had reduced her to a shadow of her former self.

*Thank God* she'd caught him cheating.

Otherwise, she might have never left. She might have never found herself again, and would be in this perpetual cycle of trying to be something for him that she would never achieve. Miserable. Small.

Pathetic.

But no more.

"We weren't right for each other, Andy," she said. "Let's just leave it at that."

She spun, and started again for her suite, but a bruising grip on her upper arm stopped her.

"You can't walk away from me, you fucking—"

Before Pepper got more than a syllable of protest out there was a *crunch*.

A crunch that was followed by cursing.

Cursing that was trailed by her whirling around and seeing Derek standing over Andy, who was cupping his face with both hands.

"Why the fuck did you do that?" Andy cried out, the words muffled by his palms.

"You don't get to touch her," Derek snapped. "Not ever."

"Been there, *done* that," he said. "Wasn't impressed."

In one smooth movement, Derek yanked Andy up by the collar then punched him in the face again.

The *crunch* this time was louder, and Pepper shuddered.

"She is an amazing woman. The best one I know—"

Andy snorted.

It sounded painful.

"If I hear you say another thing about her." Derek's foot landed on Andy's chest. *Hard*. Okay, fine, it was a kick, but a well-deserved one in her opinion. "Hell, if I hear you say her name or use that dumbass nickname of yours, then know that I will hunt you down and beat the shit out of you."

She'd never condoned violence, never wanted her man to go

all *Taken* or punch someone out because of some perceived slight against her honor, but now that it had happened, she couldn't say she regretted Derek doing it.

Andy had been cruel, and her skin burned where he'd grabbed it harshly, her shoulder ached from nearly being wrenched from its socket.

So . . . go her. Getting all bloodthirsty in her old age.

And as though the word *blood* trailing across her mind had triggered it, Andy's hands slipped away from his face.

Blood.

Oh God, he was *bleeding*.

The world went hazy.

The drama and emotion and fatigue of the day caught up with her.

She wavered.

Her knees hit the sand.

---

Pepper woke to blinding light.

"Sweetheart, are you okay?"

Her lids slid open then flashed shut just as quickly. Good God, that hurt. "Where are we?" she muttered.

"Bathroom," Derek said. "You hit your head on a rock."

She groaned. Literally the entire beach and, *of course*, she'd hit the only rock in the vicinity.

"You have a knot the size of Rhode Island on your forehead, but aside from that you're fine."

"No blood?" She cracked an eye, saw she was in the bathroom, the fluorescent lights blaring down in all their glory, and promptly slammed them shut.

Gross. Washed out. *Passed* out. All her flaws on display.

Yes, she was being ridiculous.

Yes, she knew.

"No blood," he said.

The air left her in a *whoosh*.

"Andy, on the other hand."

"Andy!" She sat up, her head tilt-a-whirling from the speed of her movement. Ninja skills she did not have. Blinking to clear the blurriness away, Pepper glanced at the mirror. Then promptly winced at the size of the lump above her eyebrow.

*That* was going to look gorgeous in wedding pictures.

"Is he okay?" she asked, gently pressing on the bump.

Derek met her gaze in the mirror. "Why would you give one iota of a fuck about that bastard?"

"Because it's Summer and my brother's wedding," she said. "And I don't want to be responsible for knocking out the best man."

"*I'm* responsible for knocking out the best man."

"That's not—"

"And I'm happy to have done so."

"Derek!"

"He hurt you."

Pepper sighed. Why was he here? Why was he pretending to care? "I hurt myself," she murmured, thinking of Derek and not Andy. "As usual."

Derek jumped up from the edge of the tub and crossed to her. "He. Hurt. You."

"I'm. Fine," she snapped.

A strange look crossed over Derek's face. It almost looked like rage, except it was gone so rapidly she could almost imagine it hadn't even been there in the first place.

"You didn't give those bruises to yourself." He placed one hand on the counter near her hip, eyes piercing as they held hers in the mirror. "Has he done that before?"

"Done what?"

Her breath caught when his other hand slid down her spine, rested on her other hip.

"Hurt you."

"No."

His body caged hers in, palm shifting to the counter, chest pressing against her back. He smelled so good, spicy and slightly tangy from the ocean air, wholly male and . . . and Derek. The man was her kryptonite, the one person in the world who'd made everything feel perfectly fine when the pieces had been falling apart. Hell, he was the one who made things seem okay when the pieces were shattered and on fire and causing the rest of the world to implode.

He—

Didn't want her.

Disgust rippled through her. So much for keeping her distance, for having her pride. Really, it shouldn't be a surprise. She'd been half in love with him since she was a teenager, lusting and idolizing him in equal measure.

*Of course*, she loved him now.

Right after he'd pulled away.

Emotionally *and* literally.

Distant and cold . . . and because after one pregnant—not her, thankfully—moment he sighed and stepped away.

"Ice on that head," he told her, picking up a washcloth and dropping some ice into the center of it. He balled the cotton, pressed it to her bump, and grabbed her hand to hold it in place.

"It's fine."

"Of course it is," he agreed, stepping back.

The ice was cold against her skin, but not as cold as the distance between them. As the space when he said, "Take care."

As the quiet click of the door when he left without another word.

# THIRTY-TWO

# BEST MAN IN TRAINING

Derek

HE WAS DOING HIS BEST.

Mainly to not kill every member of the O'Brien clan.

Paul wasn't happy that he'd nearly beaten Andy to a pulp. Peter was upset over a contract and spending every spare moment on his phone. He had no time for any of them, least of all Derek, who barely qualified on the business associate slash baby-sitter scale.

But dammit, he *needed* two minutes with Peter O'Brien. Two minutes to explain to him why their deal was off.

Two minutes to explain why he was in love with Pepper.

Dammit, he should have made that clear to Peter before he'd slept with her.

But she'd been there all gorgeous and sexy and demanding. And he'd been naked. He had no self-control when it came to Pepper O'Brien. Still, the least he could do was make his intentions plain to Peter before he flaunted their relationship before her family.

Derek knew how Peter worked. He'd take credit for the relationship, try to manipulate it for his own benefit.

Soon the pair of them would be paraded in front of daytime talk show hosts, the running joke being how capable he is of keeping Pepper from creating chaos. Let alone that the chaos—mostly—wasn't her fault, and that she tried to stay free and clear of any and all drama.

Everything would be rehashed.

He didn't want that for her.

". . . and that's final!" Peter boomed into his phone. He pulled the cell from his ear, pressed the End button, and slammed the device down onto the table. "People are fucking idiots."

People were too afraid to act because they thought Peter would lay waste to their careers, so they came to him with every potential issue.

They didn't want their asses on the line when it came to press releases or movie posters or press junkets.

Peter O'Brien was a perfectionist. A control freak.

Which made people afraid to act. Afraid to problem solve.

Which meant his cell phone never stopped ringing.

And he got off on it.

"I need to speak with you," Derek said, crossing the room.

The groomsmen were all getting ready for the next event. The rehearsal and subsequent dinner were the final items on the agenda before the wedding the following afternoon, and since he'd bloodied and bruised the best man, it was on him to take over the head groomsman duties.

Or so Paul had declared.

Not that Derek could blame the man.

But all he wanted was this wedding to be over so he and Pepper would be free of her family for a good long while. He wanted to go back to just her and him and the beach. Peace and quiet and continuing learning each other, to build something together.

"Sure, son," Peter said, in his typical condescending tone. "What do you need?"

"I have to talk to you about Pepper."

Across the room, Paul groaned. "Not my sister. What has she done this time?"

Derek shoved down a wave of annoyance. He turned to face Paul. "Pepper hasn't done *anything*."

"She did *something*," Paul muttered. "My best man is sporting a broken nose and two black eyes."

"Your best man was an asshole who deserved a lot more than that."

"Why?"

Derek turned, saw Peter's eyes were narrowed. This was so beyond the point, so far from what he wanted to discuss.

But Peter should know what a snake Andy was.

"He grabbed her. Bruised her arms." Derek thrust a hand through his hair. "She said he'd never done that before, but—"

"I will kill him." Peter's tone was deadly. Well-deserved but deadly nonetheless.

"Dad!"

Paul's tone was whiny. Well-deserved and exceptionally annoying.

"Andy doesn't matter," Derek interrupted. "I need—"

Peter's phone rang. He lifted it to his ear and immediately began talking.

Paul turned back to the mirror with a sigh.

Derek cursed inwardly.

The moment had passed. Again.

THE REHEARSAL WENT off without a hitch.

That is, if someone considered the mothers of the bride and the groom at each others' throats so frequently that the wedding planner—looking very pale but also very determined—had needed to send them to their respective corners, successful.

But they'd gotten through the rehearsal. The groomsmen and bridesmaids understood their positions. The bride had made her grand entrance—sans wedding dress, but in a very acceptable white stand-in. They'd run through vows and even practiced a "wedding kiss."

The only thing left was food.

As in they finally got to eat some.

During which Derek planned to tie down Peter O'Brien if necessary. He needed to put their deal to an end. He'd written an addendum to their contract—see, his law skills *hadn't* gone unused—and now he needed Peter to acknowledge and sign on the dotted line.

Until then, he had to keep his distance from Pepper.

She deserved someone who didn't have puppet strings attached.

She deserved more than a man who was chasing after her family's money and resources.

She deserved a man who loved her for herself, not for any of the rest of it.

"Derek."

The feminine hiss didn't belong to Pepper.

Instead it was Summer, standing opposite him, eyes glaring. What could *she* possibly want?

He'd jumped hoops, looked attentive. For fuck's sake, his mind had drifted for one second—

Then he blinked and realized what she needed.

Rings.

Because apparently they were running through the whole damned thing.

Again.

*Again.*

Please let lightning strike him down.

He'd die too young, but at least he would be done with this godforsaken rehearsal.

But unfortunately, lightning didn't come at his command, and he reached into his pocket for the rings. He only had himself to blame for having to step into Andy's duties. The other man couldn't see out of either eye, let alone appear reasonably presentable for a photographer and videographer, and God knew what other kinds of -graphers Summer and Paul had hired.

Still, Derek was half-hoping that the double black eyes healed rapidly. He was also half-hoping that Andy would fall into a vat of acid.

Simple requests. That was all he wanted.

"Derek!" Summer hissed again.

"Sorry," he muttered and pulled the rings from his pocket for the fourth time that evening.

Food. It would come soon.

# THIRTY-THREE

# WORDS HURT

Pepper

IT REALLY *WAS* a gorgeous place to get married.

Pepper stared out along the beach. The sun was just descending, a bright orange orb that hung behind her brother and Summer. They couldn't have timed the ceremony better, and the pictures—colorful sky, deep blue waves, pale sand— would be incredible.

This should have been her wedding and yet . . . she couldn't find room in her heart to be sad any longer.

Yes, she was hurt about Derek and his hot and cold, snappy then caring whiplash-like moods. Yes, her heart ached when she thought about her hope they were different and had something worthwhile to build a relationship on. Yes, the welt on her head throbbed like hell.

But no, she couldn't be sad that she'd skipped out on marrying Andy.

"And I now pronounce you man and wife," the officiant said.

Summer and Paul kissed, the small group of guests cheered, but Pepper's voice was caught in her throat.

Because . . . of Derek.

She turned away from the sight of her brother sucking face to see him watching her.

With warmth. With hope. With . . . love?

But how—?

The noise of the crowd faded, the crash of the waves disappeared. The rest of the world just fell away. It was her and Derek and—

He came to her.

Maybe he'd apologize for the distance. Perhaps she'd even understand and find a way to forgive him, to move forward. Need was heavy in his eyes as he closed the space between them.

And—

Then his face went blank.

"Let's go," he said, taking her arm and tugging her forward.

She stumbled but recovered quickly, or truthfully, Derek held her steady until she regained her footing.

"What—?"

"We need to move," he hissed.

Just that quickly, everything—the noise, the crowd, the videographer—flashed back into her mind. The sudden cacophony nearly knocked her backward.

But she was made of sterner stuff.

Straightening her spine, she walked down the sandy aisle with Derek.

Andy glared at her from the back row of chairs, raccoon eyes in full effect, bandage across the bridge of his nose. Considering the amount of concealer it had taken to cover the bruises on her arm and the goose egg on her head, she didn't feel bad.

"Come on," Derek snapped when her feet stalled again.

Her fingers tightened on his arm, nails digging deep into his skin. "Why are you being such an asshole?"

"I'm trying to do the right thing," he gritted out, hand coming over, ostensibly to cover hers, but in reality, he gripped her fingers and forced them to loosen. "And seeing you up there—"

He clamped his mouth shut, stalling the words.

Seeing her up there?

She waited until they'd passed by the photographer and were standing behind the staging area for the reception. They'd await orders for their next duties.

"What did you mean? Seeing me up there doing what?"

He shook his head, kept his stare determinedly averted.

And Pepper had had enough.

"How is treating me like crap the right thing?" she snapped, anger swelling up within her and bursting free.

"I'm—" He clenched his jaw. "I'm not treating you like—"

She snorted and he sighed, thrusting a hand through his hair. "I'm not trying to hurt you. I'm just trying to make things right."

She yanked her arm from his grip. "Yeah? By being cruel? By playing with my feelings? By pushing me away?"

"I want your father to know—"

"What?" Peter O'Brien's booming voice cut through the space between them. "What do you need me to know?"

Derek froze, eyes sliding shut for one long moment. Then he sighed and said, "The contract—"

"You play hard ball, Cashette. I offered you a damn good contract, but since you undertaking Pepper has brought about a whole slew of other complications, I'll double my contribution."

"I don't need a babysitter," Pepper said. "I put up with it because . . . well, I was weak and sad and pathetic, but Dad, you've got to stop doing this. I'm—"

She stopped talking because her father hadn't even looked at her.

He. Didn't. Look. At. Her.

Instead, he kept his gaze on Derek. "Good job romancing her. The way she looks at you." Peter laughed. "Yeah, you have her well in hand."

Derek's lids flashed open. "I—"

"Romance?" she asked.

"Pepper was—"

"Marry the girl and you'll get triple."

"That's not—"

"What do you mean *romancing?*"

Derek's eyes flicked to hers, sorrow in their depths. "Pepper. It's not what you think. I didn't—"

"Sometimes a woman needs a man to straighten her out," Peter said proudly. "And Derek is the one to do that for you. Now, about marrying—"

Then she got it.

Derek wasn't just a babysitter. Her father had paid him—or bribed him with contracts, whatever. The point was . . . her father had forced him to be with her.

Humiliation swept over her.

He'd kissed her. He'd held her. He'd had *sex* with her.

Because her father had decreed it.

Oh God. She was going to be sick.

Peter smirked. "Too soon? Well, her dowry—oh I'm sorry, I'm not supposed to mention words like that any longer. Let's just say that if you take this O'Brien girl off the market and off my hands, you'll never have to worry about contracts again."

She waited.

After everything she still actually *waited* for Derek to say something, to stand up for her, to tell her father to fuck the fuck off.

But Derek didn't.

Instead, he just stared at Peter, glancing back and forth between him and Pepper. His face was ashen, his eyes ashamed.

And that's when Pepper knew.

"This was never about us, was it?"

Derek's face hardened. "How can you say that?"

"Oh, I don't know," she ground out. "Probably because you've pulled me in and pushed me away too many times to count. Or maybe it's the fact that my father is paying you to marry me? I thought"—she shook her head—"I thought that maybe we were different. I thought you cared for me."

Derek was suddenly in her face. "I *do* care about you. Your father—"

"Will rip off your arms if you don't back off and give her some space."

"We're—"

Pepper stepped away from Derek and turned to face her father.

"This is not 1840," Pepper snapped. "And I'm not some scandal you need to take care of. I don't get how you can care about my physical well-being but not give a shit about my emotional—"

"Language."

"I don't fucking care about my language," she said. "I don't care about anything. I just want—" Her voice cracked when she saw derision cross his face. It didn't matter what she wanted. He would never, *ever* get it. "I can fight my own battles," she said after clearing her throat. "I'm not a child any longer."

"You're acting like one," Peter intoned.

It would always be like this. She would never be an adult in her father's eyes, never be worthy and mature or beautiful and accomplished.

She was just Pepper. She would always be *just Pepper*.

And while that wasn't good enough for the O'Briens—or apparently for Derek—it was finally good enough for her.

It *had* to be.

She couldn't continue to live her life otherwise. Not when she was worried about stepping one toe out of line. Or panicked that she would screw up again.

Because . . . the more she freaked out, the more havoc she wreaked.

Train wrecks—at least in the form of Oscar-winning actors ending up with broken noses and Ferraris crashing through movie sets—happened when she was stressed.

Oh, she was klutzy as hell and would probably always be injuring herself, but that was okay.

She. Was. Okay.

She just wasn't perfect.

And finally, she was realizing that was okay, too.

"Pepper," Derek began.

"No." A harsh word as she took a step away from her father, from Derek and the rest of the bridal party. "Not now."

The wedding planner had pulled Summer and Paul to the side and was positioning them as they took photographs.

The bridal party would be next.

She was going to hold it together for the pictures, for the night. And then she was done.

"Sweetheart," Derek said. "It's not like you think."

She whirled around, ready to give him a set of black eyes that rivaled Andy's, but the planner, still looking remarkably pale from her bout with food poisoning, called them over. They took a multitude of pictures, ate many courses of meals. She gave a toast that didn't end in disaster, participated in a half dozen dances with the male members of the wedding party, and one unfortunate coed rendition of the electric slide. Even the bouquet toss was relatively uneventful, despite a bridesmaid—not her for a change—ending up with a black eye.

Hey, just because she ducked didn't mean it was her fault.

By the end of the night, she'd seen a tipsy Summer and Paul off on their little decorated electric cart—driver included, of course. She'd made sure gifts were packed away, that they stayed paired with their respective cards. Hell, Pepper even ensured that Uncle Ike got his drunk ass back to his suite.

Only then did she leave the festivities.

But instead of going to her room, to sit down and cry because her heart felt shredded, she walked along the beach.

The moon was full, but after the lanterns and candles and twinkly lights, it still took her eyes awhile to adjust. She spotted the dock she'd seen earlier, only this time instead of being crowded with boats and fishermen, it was empty. She stopped, brushed her soles free of sand, and picked her way to the end. The wooden planks were warm and rough beneath her bare feet as she walked its length. Water swooshed against the wooden pylons, a rhythmic *swish-swash*, that soothed her as she sat and dangled her legs over the edge, finally letting the emotions free.

Derek was her conundrum, and she didn't know what to do.

She shouldn't be mad. He'd made it clear time and again that her father was the reason he was in Stoneybrook. Hell, he'd said her father was the reason he was babysitting in her in the first place.

The problem was . . .

She sighed, laid back. The problem was that *she'd* started thinking that things were different. She'd forgotten she was an assignment, a stepping-stone from one place to the next.

She'd fallen in love.

With someone who couldn't love her back.

Now her feelings were hurt—shattered—and what was she going to do about it?

Mope? Run crying to her father?

Pepper snorted.

Yeah, that was never going to happen again.

"You always did think you were a comedian."

# THIRTY-FOUR

# THE AFOREMENTIONED TRAIN WRECK

SHE SAT bolt upright at those words.

Masculine. Fierce. Shiver-inducing.

Unfortunately the wrong kind of shudder.

"An-Andy," she said. The expression on his face made her immediately scoot away from him, nearly toppling herself off the edge of the dock. "What are you doing here?"

His face somehow went even darker, crueler. "No knight in shining armor to save you this time."

Her throat went dry. "I—"

In the movies her father produced, there would have been a huge buildup of music, some cuts between her face and Andy's —obviously the villain in this piece. All would have served the purpose of driving up the tension in the flick.

That tension was unnecessary.

Her heart already pounded. A cold sweat had broken out on her skin. She quaked when a cold gust of ocean air sluiced across the moisture.

So yeah, she had plenty of tension.

Carefully, she pushed to her feet. "Did you need something?"

Andy laughed, but it wasn't a nice one. "You're kidding, right? You embarrass me, and *that's* what you're asking? I *needed* something six months ago when I lost the contract with your father."

She frowned, took a cautious step sideways, trying to inch herself away from the end of the dock.

Her ex was unhinged, and there was no other word for it. Aside from the facial injuries, courtesy of Derek, Andy's hair was mussed, his shirt wrinkled, his eyes wild and dilated.

The moonlight showed all of that clearly.

And even from this distance, his alcohol breath rivaled even that of Uncle Ike's.

Drunk. Angry. Disturbed.

Not the combination she wanted to be facing on a normal day, but most especially not with the bruises on her arm still aching and her shoulder throbbing in memory of his clutching, pain-inducing grip.

"I don't know anything about my father's contracts," she said. Then hurried to add when his eyes sparked angrily, "But I'm sure I could mention something and—"

"What? I'd be forever grateful?" Andy sneered. "You screwed me out a deal that would have brought millions, and now your new fuck buddy is getting the benefits? No." His fingers went to the waistband of his slacks. "If *fucking* you is all that it takes to secure O'Brien funding then—"

"There's nothing between Derek and me, Andy," she said. Not anymore. "We're just . . ." Fuck, what were they? "Friends."

"Lies!" He unbuckled his belt, sliding it from the loops and tossing it to the dock where it landed with an ominous rattle. "I've seen the way you look at him. It's obvious he's stuck his—"

"Andy!" she snapped. "Enough. We were over when you cheated on me. I can't be with someone who isn't faithful."

"*No one* in our circle is faithful."

She sighed. "That doesn't make it right."

"That doesn't make it all wrong, either," he said. "I can forgive you for sleeping with the lawyer, but when we get back together" —he undid the button on his slacks, slid down the zipper—"*that* needs to be over. I'm not sharing with the fucking bastard."

He was insane.

And he wasn't listening or getting that they would never be a *them* or a *we* again. That they were done. Had been done.

But Andy had never been a good listener.

His hands found the buttons of his shirt.

"Stop," she said, taking another step sideways. She was in the middle of the dock, five feet from freedom, and yet she would have to pass close to Andy to gain it. The pier was narrow and rickety, a row of simple wooden slats where the fishermen cleaned their catch after a long day at sea.

"No," he muttered. "I have to fuck you. Then you'll see." He wavered. "Then *he'll* see—"

His shirt landed in a crumpled pile on the dock. He lifted his hands to the waistband of his slacks—

And Pepper knew she had to act.

It was either that or just stand there and wait for this idiocy he thought made sense to come to a head. Drunk or not, she didn't think she could fight him off.

So, she made a run for it, darting past Andy for the beach.

"Hey!"

She watched as he whirled. His slacks fell from his grip, bunching at his ankles, gathering above his shoes.

"Goddammit," he said, trying to toe the loafers off and move after her.

Loafers, such a terrible fashion choice for men. So uppity. So—

*Splash.*

"Holy mother of tampons," she blurted.

One second Andy had been stumbling along the dock after her, the next he was in the water.

A drunk man was in the water.

He'd drown.

She took a step toward the edge of the dock, ready to jump in after him.

A pair of firm hands stopped her.

That was when the screaming began.

---

THE ONLY GOOD thing to come out of the aftermath of Summer and Paul's wedding was that the aforementioned pair had already departed the island.

They didn't have to deal with police reports. Or dead bodies.

Because Andy had stumbled upon shark-infested waters.

Quite literally had *fallen* into them.

Turned out that the fishermen tended to throw the unfavorable bits of their catch into the water next to the dock at the end of the day. Just past sunset, most every day.

The sharks had been trained to return to the dock day in and day out. Even on those days when the fishermen weren't allowed to clean their catch.

Like event days.

Like *wedding* days.

Andy, unfortunately, had stumbled into an aggressive, *hungry* group of tiger sharks.

And Andy hadn't found his way out.

Pepper felt guilty.

Okay, she didn't feel *horribly* guilty. He hadn't been stripping down for innocent reasons, hadn't been about to make an attempt at wooing her through naked moonlight dancing.

He would have tried to rape her.

His fall meant he hadn't had the chance to do so.

She was almost grateful he'd done it to himself.

Especially when the news came out of his embezzling.

His company was tanking because he'd gambled away funds from contracts with production groups, O'Brien films included, money that was supposed to have gone to script development.

Turned out, the writers he'd contracted had never been paid.

She could only assume that he'd been hoping to bully her back into a relationship. That he'd force himself on her, and that would somehow bring her in line so he could get new contracts, new cash to fuel his addiction.

He hadn't counted on Derek.

He hadn't expected her to have moved on. To fight. To not just give in.

And considering the pathetic creature she'd been in their relationship, that wouldn't have been too far off.

Thank God, she'd finally found her backbone.

# THIRTY-FIVE

# WHITE KNIGHT SYNDROME

Derek

HE STARED out the window of the plane and tried to figure out how it had all gone so fucking wrong.

He was in love with Pepper O'Brien, and she wanted nothing to do with him.

He'd hand delivered the new contract to her father that morning, forced both of them to sign on the dotted line even when Peter had protested, and was now free of the O'Brien influence.

His movie would be made on his terms, his way and—

Pepper was gone.

As in, her suite was empty, the family's private jet commandeered, gone.

She'd left, and he'd fucked up. Royally.

Derek Cashette had a hero complex. He'd wanted to ride in and save the day from her family. To provide a grand gesture that showed how much he loved her, while demonstrating to her father and brother that she was special and important and—

Dammit. None of that mattered now.

Pepper was confused and hurt, and if he'd just taken a minute to explain everything instead of trying to white knight it, he wouldn't be riding coach on a red eye flight back to Stoneybrook.

The flight was long and as those things went, delayed by several hours. He'd sat next to a bull of a man who'd hogged the shared armrest and smelled liked he'd taken up eating raw onions. His luggage—which he'd been forced to gate check due to a lack of overhead bin space—was lost.

No taxis were at the stand. His cell was dead and he couldn't call a Lyft.

All things considered, *he* was the train wreck.

It was after midnight by the time he'd driven into the outskirts of Stoneybrook. Later still, when he'd parked at Pepper's house.

No lights were on in her house, but he wasn't going to let that slow him down. He retrieved the spare key, let himself in, and—

Nothing.

She wasn't there.

Funny how he could tell that without taking more than a single step through the front door.

But Pepper was spirit and life and energy. And at that moment, her cottage didn't have any.

She'd taken the plane, could be anywhere in the world.

"I thought you might show up."

He turned and saw Shannon standing in the doorway.

"Where is she?"

A shrug. "She asked that I not say anything."

"Shannon—"

She flicked on a light. "Seems like you screwed up majorly on that little island of paradise."

"A man died. I couldn't—"

"I think you know that you screwed up long before that." She nodded at the sheaf of papers in his hand. "I think you were keeping secrets—good ones, maybe—but secrets that still hurt her."

"I wanted to show her that she meant more."

A flash of emotion crossed Shannon's face, and Derek knew his words were a painful reminder of her asshole of a husband. Not that he was much different. He'd been an asshole to Pepper. Not sharing. Not telling her what was going on when he promised, first and foremost, to be honest. "A woman deserves to know that she means something."

"I don't disagree with you," she murmured.

He released a breath. Now she would tell him—

"But I'm still not telling you where Pepper is."

"Shannon!" he snapped.

"Don't try and use Mom Voice on me," she snapped back, crossing her arms. "I've perfected the act, mister. I'm not breaking my promise to her. She's had very few people in her life who can say that and I'm not going to ruin our friendship and trust, just because you found a conscience."

"Fuck," he muttered, thrusting a hand through his hair and starting for the door.

"But," she said, stepping back. "I think if you look around and discover what's missing, you'll know where she went." With a wave, she turned away and closed the door.

"Shannon . . ." he began then trailing off.

It was pointless. He knew she could out-stubborn him any day of the week. He'd seen her easily stare down Rylie when the six-year-old was giving puppy dog eyes for an ice cream.

And win.

He would have caved within ten seconds.

"Fuck," he muttered again, knowing that he was lucky

enough that she'd given him *something*, even if it wasn't the *something* he'd been hoping for.

A scavenger hunt through Pepper's cottage instead of her location.

But it was something.

Yeah, it got him twenty minutes of walking through each room of the house finding the furniture in its proper locations, her bedroom floor filled with a scattering of clothes and necklaces that was normal, the kitchen—

*Here* he got a little niggle.

Something wasn't quite right.

But the fridge was full of food, the sink cleared of dishes. Four chairs, one table. The sink, though, something was off about the metal basin. He crossed the room and peered down. Aside from a rogue spoon, there was nothing but water-spotted stainless steel. A sponge, a bottle of dish soap—

*Oh.*

The sculpture was gone.

Derek ran his fingers across the windowsill above the sink, the surface slightly rough with leftover sand.

She'd taken her sculpture. He hurried to the family room, saw several blank spots on the shelves. Spots that had once held more of her art work. But that still didn't explain anything. She'd taken the pieces somewhere. *Great.* She could quite literally be anywhere.

Well, not Antarctica and probably not the Midwest or sub-Saharan Africa. But a busy metropolitan—New York, London, Paris, San Francisco—pick his poison and she might be there.

New York was closest, he decided, and so he would start there.

Derek had pulled his phone from his pocket, ready to book another flight when he noticed a white triangle poking out from beneath the throw rug in the front hall.

He bent, lifted the woven material, and saw it was a business card.

For a gallery in San Francisco.

Change of plans.

The card went into his wallet as he pulled open the browser on his phone and booked a flight to the City by the Bay.

# THIRTY-SIX
# UNDERDRESSED

Pepper

SHE STARED at the gorgeous man across from her. He was ruggedly handsome in a Jason-Momoa-do-me-now sort of way. Beard, tats, perfectly fitted suit. She wanted to call it maroon because her brain recognized it was near that shade.

Except maroon didn't do the man in front of her justice. He was plum or ruby or claret.

Yes, that was the perfect description. A crisp white shirt paired with the crisp reddish purples of a glass of . . . well, claret.

"These are absolutely brilliant, aren't they Sara?" He prodded the gorgeous nugget of petite blondness next to him with his elbow. "How much? Six grand?"

Pepper's throat closed up.

Her teeny tiny slapped together piece of glass and driftwood and shells was going to be priced at six *thousand* dollars?

What in the what?

"At least that much," Sara said.

"Are you Sara Jetty?" Pepper couldn't help but asking. She

didn't fan girl over much, but she had watched some of the big figure skating competitions. Sara Jetty had been right around her age when she'd won her gold medal.

Though . . . it had been taken away, after her former coaches had accused Sara of cheating, and only recently returned.

Why it had taken ten years for the truth to come to light, Pepper didn't know. She was only glad that one of her childhood heroes—turned talented artist—had been cleared of all wrongdoing.

"It's Sara Stewart now," Sara said. "But, yes. I'm that Sara."

Mitch smirked, nudged her again. "Always infamous."

"Not quite so much anymore."

Pepper glanced around at the gallery's walls as they teased each other. "And those are"—she stood, crossed to a rendering of the Golden Gate bridge, done in shades of gray with the barest hint of copper—"*that* is incredible," she breathed.

"It's yours," Sara said from behind her shoulder.

Pepper jumped, not having heard the other woman come over. She'd been lost in the swirls of fog, the twisting wires of the span, the flecks of cars as they drove across. "Wh-what?"

Sara grinned. "I mean you can have it. So long as you promise to eventually make me a sculpture in return."

She gulped. How could she ever hope that her artwork could possibly compare to Sara's? She was a novice with no practical experience. Her degree in art history could hardly be a suitable substitute for real, hands-on training.

"I had that look," Sara said. "The I'm-not-worthy, I-can't-compare one you're sporting now." She stopped, waited until Pepper met her eyes. "Here's the thing. I'm not a bull-shitter. If I say your stuff is good, it's good. Your first piece for six grand? That'll sell like the last chocolate bar at a Sugar Anonymous meeting."

"But—"

"Shh, honey," Mitch said. "I gave little Ms. Stewart this talk not too long ago and I want a front row seat for her version of my brilliance."

"You're terrible," Sara told him, swatting at his arm. "But I love you anyway."

"I know." Mitch laughed. "No, keep going, sweetie. I think this one is smart enough to get it on the first go around."

"I resent that comment," Sara said with a chuckle that made Mitch laugh again. Then she went on, "The bottom line is that you deserve something good in your life. I've probably seen your name come up as frequently as mine in the gossip columns, but that doesn't define you." A pause. "You're *not* the words they assign to you."

Pepper thought of the newspaper article she'd seen only that morning. *Train Wreck in Tahiti*, the latest scoop on the death of Pepper O'Brien's ex-fiancé.

She'd made it almost too easy for the paparazzi this time.

"And I think you know that," Sara said firmly. "I think you're starting to understand that exact thing."

Pepper's mouth turned up. "It took me long enough."

Mitch squeezed her arm. "The important thing is that you got there. It took me a long time to think I was worthy, but then I met Marcus and—"

*Damn.*

Pepper sighed.

The good ones were always—

"What did I say?" Mitch asked.

"Nothing," Sara said, patting her on the shoulder. "Pepper just realized you were gay." In a stage whisper she added, "He gets that a lot."

"In fairness," Pepper replied, "he's pretty much the hottest man I've seen in my life—"

Somewhere in the back of her mind, she'd registered the

tinkle of the bell as the door to the gallery opening, but hadn't actually processed that someone might be walking into the shop.

Which meant that Derek's voice made her jump.

"The *hottest* man?"

Growly. Definitely irritated and growling and pissed off.

Derek.

Who was rumpled and pissed and—

*Derek.*

She sighed. God, she loved him. Pathetic. Yes, she realized that with crystal clear accuracy.

But—

Mitch slid in front of her, eyed Derek up and down. "Can I help you?" There was a note of warning in his voice, and considering that Derek looked as though he'd been pulled backward through a car wash, Pepper appreciated the show of male concern.

"I'm here to see Pepper," he said, sidestepping in an attempt to move past Mitch. Who quickly adjusted his position to stay between them.

Mitch crossed his arms. "You stay over there and talk."

"We don't have anything to talk about anyway," Pepper muttered. "You made things clear."

"I didn't make anything clear," Derek snapped. "I was trying to make things right with your father."

Oh, *that* was rich. He was worried about her father's opinion of him and his contract. She rolled her eyes. "I know all about your relationship with my father, thank you very much. Just leave, Derek. I won't do anything to affect your contract."

Not that it would make any bit of difference anyway.

Her opinion wasn't exactly high on her father's list.

"I don't *have* a contract with your father. Not any longer."

A twisting feeling began in her stomach, tying her insides tighter and tighter. So *that* was why he was there.

To get his contract back.

The small bud of hope she'd felt at seeing him—come on, she was an intrinsically optimistic person—shriveled and died.

"I'll talk to my father," she said quietly. "See if I can do some press or something in exchange for a new one."

"That's not what I *want!*" Derek all but shouted.

"I don't know what else you *do* want!" she shouted back. "Not me. Not my body. Not my heart. It's—"

"I want everything," he said. "Every piece of you. Your heart, your soul, your—"

"Sweet, sweet ass," Mitch interjected with a snort.

"Shut up," Sara hissed.

Too late, Pepper thought. *All* of it was too late. She started to take a step back and stopped, heaven forbid she collide with some priceless—okay, she was in gallery—*expensive* piece of art.

Look at her, growing up. Making a difference. Saving the world.

If saving the world could be called protecting artwork from her particular brand of calamity.

"I don't want a contract with your father," Derek said. "I don't give a damn about him. I want you."

"Ding. Ding. Ding," Mitch said. "Now *that's* the ticket. Keep going, man."

"No," Pepper said, eyes flicking toward him. "It's *not* the ticket." Then her gaze went back to Derek. "Maybe once. Maybe once I could have forgiven you. But . . . you wounded me, you made me hope and just sliced me to pieces. So maybe I love you right now, but that'll change. I'll get over it and I'll come out stronger on the other side."

And as Derek stood there, face clouding with an emotion she didn't want to see—pity? dismay? empathy?—Pepper sprinted out the door, the tinkling bell cheerfully obscene behind her.

# THIRTY-SEVEN

# BANANAS. IT'S ALL B-A-N-A-N-A-S, BANANAS

SHE GOT all of three steps before Derek stopped her.

"Wait," he said.

"No!" Her heart pounded, bile burned the back of her throat. She was going to throw up. Seriously, she was going to puke all over him, and then it would show up on some gossip show and—

"Sweetheart . . ."

His tone did it. The soft, don't-scare-the-frightened-animal version. As though she might—fine—*had* run.

Her eyes were damp. "Why can't you just leave me alone?"

"Because I love you, too."

One tear fell. Then another. She shook her head.

"Come here." Derek didn't give her a chance to refuse, just tucked his arm around her and led her into the shop.

"Back room," she heard Mitch say distantly, since the dam had apparently broken and she was crying hard.

"I'm—"

"Hush now," Derek said. "Just wait."

They walked through another doorway. This room was

nothing like the front of the store, filled to the brim with boxes, lit with ugly fluorescent bulbs.

Not that it mattered. Because no matter how hard she tried to ignore him, her eyes wouldn't drift from Derek for more than a few seconds.

He was tall. He was gorgeous.

She was pathetically in love with him.

"I love you," he said again.

It couldn't be true. He *had* to want something. Or this had to be some plan of her father's.

This *wasn't* real.

And, fuck it all, she deserved something so much better.

She needed someone to love her for *her*. She was worthy and important and—

Derek pulled out his phone. A bitter part of her half-expected him to start recording her, to sell her tears for front-page fodder.

That part was disappointed when she heard the metallic ring of FaceTime.

Her father's voice blared out through the speakers.

"Derek," he said jovially, "I knew you would see reason."

"Tell her," Derek growled, pointing the phone in Pepper's direction.

A pause.

"Cashette—"

"If you love your daughter even a little bit," he gritted out. "You'll give her this."

"Of course I love her," Peter said. "She's my blood—"

"Then. Tell. Her!"

Pepper listened to the conversation from a distance, not understanding, pulse still pounding and hope, such a tender filament of the toxic emotion, unfurling in her heart.

The phone was thrust into her hands. Peter O'Brien's face was in hers.

And suddenly she was that little girl again. She needed reassurance but her father wouldn't be the one to provide it.

He never had.

So why would this time be different?

But . . . this time something *was* different because Peter sighed, his brows pulled down in frustration. "Derek tried to reach me for weeks to cancel his contract."

His tone wasn't comforting.

The words were though.

Her eyes flicked over to Derek. He nodded.

"How many?" she asked softly. It wasn't really directed at her father, because things were finally making sense.

"How should I know?" Peter boomed.

Derek grabbed the phone, pressed the little red button and her father disappeared from sight.

Thank God.

"Since the first night," Derek said, one dimple making a quick appearance. "Well, after the stomach flu from hell concluded." He set the phone on a box and took a step closer to her. "Pepper . . ."

"What?" she asked.

"I need—" He shook his head. "Please let me hold you."

Her breath caught. She knew the moment his arms went around her, she would be done for. This resistance, the barely formed wall would crumble like sand. Given time, she might heat that sand into glass, make it stronger, make it more impermeable.

But she had the feeling that Derek would always be able to get through.

"Please?"

Pepper nodded, and then she was in his arms.

How did the simple act of being held by another person make all the difference? She was centered, safe . . . cherished.

And *that* was the difference.

More so than any other person in the world, when Derek held her, she felt cherished.

"I didn't know you. At first, I didn't understand." His forehead came to rest on hers, breath puffing against her lips, minty and sweet, and she was overwhelmed with the desire to close the distance between their mouths. To take that sweetness inside her and let it fill her up. But he was still talking. "I know now," he said. "I get why we've always had that pull. Why my eyes always tracked you, even though I was supposed to be hanging out with your brother. You have this light about you, sweetheart. It's why people watch you so closely."

She snorted.

His lips twitched. "And it's not the disasters. You've got this pureness inside, joy in the simple things, a desire to help. It kills me to see how hard people try to stamp that out of you."

"*I* make the disasters," she said. "If I was more careful. Better at staying focused and not getting off track—"

"They would only find something else to pull apart."

Pepper sighed. "You know what they've called me. I'm the *Train Wreck in—*"

"No," he said, hand coming up to grip the back of her neck. "You're *mine.*"

Why did that declaration make her all shivery?

She snorted. Because Derek was Derek.

"Deny it all you want," he said. "I don't want you cracking me in the head with an Oscar, or"—he glanced around at the boxes of art surrounding them—"a sculpture of Aphrodite—"

It was her turn to look around, to spy the piece he'd eyed.

She promptly rolled hers.

"Seriously?" she asked. "An entire room and you pick the naked statue?"

"She has giant—"

"You're ruining it," she muttered.

A smile teased the corners of his lips. "How can I save it?"

"Kiss me."

His face softened, his other hand came up and cupped her jaw. "Now *that* I can do."

When his lips met hers, Pepper felt complete. Which was sappy as hell, but also the truth. Derek was the one person in the world who understood her, probably better than she understood herself.

The kiss was short—or well, shorter than she wanted it to be. But his words after made up for it.

"I tried to cancel the contract because I didn't want your father to have a hold over us. I didn't want us to be anything except . . . *us.*" He cupped her cheek. "I knew I was falling for you and I wanted to have us free and clear so that I could show the world that you're wonderful and perfect for me and . . . *mine.*"

She snorted. "I'm not perfect."

"Why is *that* the one thing you hear?" he asked softly. "I didn't say you were perfect. I said, you're perfect for *me*. And I realize now that I should have just talked to you, that me telling you how much you meant didn't have to be this big production or something to be done in front of your family to prove everyone wrong about you." He sighed. "*They* don't matter. You do. It should have just been me and you and what we were building, and I'm so, *so* sorry I ruined that."

She inhaled deeply then admitted the truth pinging around her heart, "It's not ruined."

"I—" He shook his head.

"It is a little dinged around the edges," she told him, "I won't deny that. But . . . just because it's something that someone would call damaged, doesn't mean it can't still be the start of something. The pieces can still come together to make something beautiful and breathtaking."

His eyes slid closed. "How could you possibly forgive me enough to give me the chance to prove we can be beautiful and breathtaking?"

"Because, setting aside your need to make a grand gesture," she murmured, winding her arms around his neck and holding him close, "I think that you're pretty much perfect for *me*, too."

His breath caught. His eyes flew open. "I'm so sorry—"

She kissed him, hard and hot and wet, long enough that she forgot all about why she was in the studio in the first place. She wanted Derek. And she wanted him now.

But he didn't forget why she was there.

He remembered.

And that made all the difference.

"Go," he murmured, stepping back, chest heaving, eyes clouded with pleasure. "Close your deal so we can go home."

She raised a brow. "You're awfully presumptuous, Mr. Cashette."

"About the deal?" He grinned. "Or me moving in?"

Her heart swelled, that hope a helium balloon inside her soul. "Both."

His fingers squeezed the back of her neck, his other hand slid down and caressed the curve of her ass. "I bet I could convince you to give me a few drawers," he murmured.

Her hand did a little walking of its own. "I bet *I* could convince you that you only need one."

He laughed. "I'm sure you could."

"Easy." She smirked.

"Damn right."

"I love you," she said. "I don't know how this is going to work out. What my family will—"

"This about you and me." He crouched a little to meet her eyes straight on. "And I don't know how this will work out, either. But I *do* know I want to figure it out with you by my side."

Just that simply her nerves settled. No pressure. No requirements. Just her and Derek and a shot at something special.

"My eyes are closed!" a voice, Mitch, called out. "I just need—"

"You're safe," Pepper said with a laugh.

Mitch made a noise that sounded disappointed. "I always miss the good stuff."

"Go," Derek murmured. "Get that deal, baby."

Her hands had somehow gotten clenched in his shirt. She released and smoothed the cotton.

"You'll wait?"

Derek brushed his mouth across hers, whispered. "Always."

# EPILOGUE

## PART ONE, TINY DISASTERS

Derek, One year later

"HOW DID we not know she was pregnant?" Derek asked.

Pepper shrugged, eyes on their newly adopted cat—now surrounded by a half dozen kittens of various colors and patterns. "The rescue said she was just fat."

They'd obviously made a rookie mistake.

And, speaking of patterns, his shirts had new ones.

He winced, and Pepper's cheeks flared hot. "I'm sorry I forgot to drop off your dry cleaning."

"I see that," he said dryly, studying the nest the mama cat had made out of his dirty dress shirts Pepper had piled next to the bed to drop off earlier that day.

Not T-shirts, of course. But expensive button-downs.

Button-downs she'd forgotten all about because she'd been working on a new sculpture and it had totally slipped her mind.

But not the cat's.

Apparently, that pile was the best place to have her kittens.

"I love you," he said and kissed Pepper's cheek. She was

covered in paint and sand and glue, her hair disheveled, her clothes torn and stained.

She was beautiful.

She was his . . . as much as he was hers.

"Just next time, take me up on my offer to drop off my own shirts." He pressed a kiss to her temple. "How's the piece?"

Her mouth split into a wide smile. "Done. Finally." A pause. "How was the meeting?"

"Over." He grinned. "They're going to distribute it."

Pepper's shriek of joy made the mama cat hiss.

"Sorry," she whispered to it, standing up and backing away carefully from the angry feline and her teeny tiny babies. "How many theaters?"

He told her.

This time her shriek was muffled by her hand. "That's amazing!"

Derek was puffed up with pride, full on peacock, and he didn't even care. His film, his dream was complete and would be in theaters. It was unbelievable.

The process had been so much harder than he'd anticipated.

But he'd done it.

On his own.

No. With Pepper by his side.

"Come outside and celebrate?" he asked. "I ordered in."

"Of course," she said. "Let me just change."

Derek put his hands on her hips and tugged her close. "I like you just like this."

"I'm not wearing a bra," she protested, though her body was already melting, brushing against his.

His fingers slipped beneath the hem of her T-shirt. "Even better."

She smacked them down. "You're impossible."

"You love me."

Her hand brushed his jaw. "I do."

"Good." He tugged her to the front of the house. "Come on."

The cottage's windows were open, the soft sound of the ocean drifting inside. He held the door for Pepper, smiled when Shannon and Rylie waved from their own deck.

Rylie was practically jumping with glee.

"She's in a good mood," Pepper said. "I wonder—"

"Dessert first," Derek said and handed her a skewer with a marshmallow on it. The fire was already going. He'd started it before going into the house, leaving Shannon and Rylie on fire-watch duty.

"Really?" Pepper asked. "You don't usually do sweets."

"But you do," he said. "Plus, it's summer. What's summer without s'mores?"

"Good point." She put her skewer into the flames.

Derek waited, holding his own with sweaty palms. It wouldn't take long, Pepper liked her marshmallows barely toasted and then—

"Want to come over?" she called to Rylie and Shannon, marshmallow still in the flames.

It was turning from white to slightly brown. Derek swallowed. That was fine, everything was good.

"No!" Shannon called back. "We're good!"

At the same time Rylie shouted, "Yes!"

"Sweetheart," Derek began.

The marshmallow was turning gray. Nope. Now it was black.

He started to reach for the skewer.

Pepper pulled back. "Mine," she scolded.

"It's—"

And there it went.

The blackened ball of sugar caught on fire.

Derek lurched to his feet, grabbed for the stick.

"Hey!" Pepper protested. "That's mine—"

She jerked backwards and . . . there it went.

A little inferno of gelatin and sugar, spinning through the air and landing in the sand with a soft *plunk*.

Pepper huffed out a breath and glared. "Really?"

"It was on fire."

"I had it under control." When he started for the stairs, she said, "Just leave it for the birds."

Yeah *that* was what he was worried about.

Already, the pesky seagulls were heading for the marshmallow.

He beat them to it, swiping up the sticky, sandy mess.

Turned out this—like his other grand gestures—was not well thought out.

But at least the marshmallow was so thoroughly torched that he didn't have trouble finding the ring inside.

Proposal by s'mores.

It had seemed so romantic in theory.

In actuality . . .

Not so much.

Pepper came down the steps and stopped before him.

Since he was already kneeling, he didn't bother to get up.

"What in the blazes—" She stopped, plunked her hands on her hips and finally took a good look at him. "Are you all right?"

He grinned. *This* woman.

"I love you," he said and held up the ring.

She stared at the sticky, dirty diamond for a long moment. Then her lips twitched. "You didn't . . ."

He nodded. "I did."

"Oh, Lord," she said.

"I know." He raised a brow. "So how about it? Make an honest man out of me?"

"Clean it first, and then we'll talk." She faked like she was going to walk away then dropped to her knees in front of him and threw her arms around his neck.

They were laughing as they kissed.

And laughter, Derek thought, wasn't a bad way to start a future.

---

Finn

He knocked on the door of the cute little bungalow that was next to his, a pail of sand toys in his hand. It was around lunchtime, and he was met with an adorable face peeking through the glass panel, its paisley curtain shoved carelessly to the side.

Freckles on a nose.

Eyes more brown than blue.

"Mom!" she yelled. "It's a man!"

"Grab your book and take it onto the deck, honey. You need to finish up your summer reading," came a female voice—not yelling, but still clearly heard because the windows along the front of the house were open to let in the fresh ocean air.

The little girl made a face but stepped back from the door, and Finn heard the pounding of footsteps on the floor.

A few seconds later, the knob turned, and a woman stood in front of him.

Gut punch.

The pain in her eyes was a fist to the stomach, hurting like hell, stealing his breath, burning through him.

And yet, she was beautiful.

Not a hair out of place. Her body was clad in a pretty blouse and form-fitting jeans, but with bare feet, a pop of red on her toes, on her lips. She looked more model than mom in the pale pink silk with long, dark hair flowing down her back in shining waves. His fingers itched to stroke, if only to prove to himself that the locks would be as soft as they looked. A cluster of bracelets on her arm clinked together as she lifted a hand, shielding her startling blue eyes from the sun.

Insane.

He saw beauty all the time, worked with some of the most beautiful females on the planet. That this woman should arrest some part of him, render him frozen in inaction just staring at her, when he was quite literally trained to always have a sound-bite, to always be charming—

He was literally losing his mind.

But then again, that was why he was here, wasn't it?

Well, not in front of this actual house, but in Stoneybrook in the first place.

An actor has one meltdown . . .

"Hi," she said, startling blue eyes careful. "Are you . . . um . . . new in town?"

He opened his mouth, holding up the bucket, when the little girl he'd seen in the window came barreling through, book clutched in one hand, stuffed fox in the other, and nearly knocking him over.

The girl was fast *and* strong.

"Whoa," he said, rocking back.

"Sorry!" she called, skidding her way to a deck chair.

"Rylie."

Just her name. In a tone that brokered no argument, but wasn't raised in volume or tinted with anger.

Model. Mom. Superhero.

This woman could be all three.

Rylie stopped, set her things down, then came over wearing a guilty expression on her face. "I'm sorry I ran into you, Mr.—"

"Stoneman," he said, filling in the blank and not considering that it was bad for him to have given his real name when he was supposed to be in the tiny East Coast town hiding and quote-unquote-finding himself while on his break for 'exhaustion' (direct quote there, from his publicist). "Finn Stoneman."

"Mr. Stoneman," Rylie repeated.

He glanced from the eyes beneath him—blue with streaks of brown—to those next to him—the arresting clear blue of a summer's sky—and hesitated for a moment, not sure what to say. But there wasn't any recognition in the mom-slash-model-slash-superhero's eyes—and not to be an arrogant asshole, but how was that even possible with his face on every magazine, every news site, every morning TV show? When his name had carried many of the big blockbuster films of the last decade? Still, he figured he'd better get his shit together and stop thinking so hard, because if Rylie was anything like his nieces and nephews, then he would only have her attention for another zero-point-three seconds.

So, he crouched down, met her gaze straight on, and said, "Thanks for apologizing. I'm not hurt."

Clunky, definitely.

But his sister hated when someone told her kids, "It's okay," when she corrected them for their behavior, saying it undermined what they could learn in that moment.

Whether or not he agreed with his sister wasn't in question —though, for the record, he thought she made a valuable point— one he'd taken, promising himself he'd make sure to use the knowledge for good.

Rylie glanced at her mother, who nodded with an encouraging smile, then ran back over to the chair, picked up her book, and started reading.

"Thanks for that," she murmured, still no recognition, which was just . . . ego popping? Amazing? Confusing? A breath of fresh air? Finn had constantly been recognized every-where he went for years now, and he didn't quite know how to respond to someone not knowing who he was.

So, yeah, ego-diminishing.

"She's a ball of energy sometimes," the woman murmured, eyes on her daughter, "and hasn't quite learned to control her body. Thank you for being so great with her."

Finn smiled. "My nieces and nephews are the same. Tiny maniacs, the lot of them."

Her expression warmed. "Oh?"

"I'm one of five kids," he told her. "The middle child with both a sister and brother on either side of me. Only my older siblings have kids though. A *lot* of them."

"Define a *lot*."

He grinned.

"I have four nephews and two nieces, ranging from ten to three."

"Okay." Her brows lifted. "That is . . ."

"A lot?" he teased and grinned. "You should see us at our family dinners." He laughed. "I swear, my parents' neighbors would hate us if they weren't invited to eat the feast my mom cooks up every Sunday."

"*Every* Sunday?" Her eyes widened.

Finn laughed. "I can tell by your face that you think it's a lot," he teased. "And you'd be right. It *is* a lot. But they're my family, and I love them." A beat. "Plus, not all of us always get together. Whoever's in town or not busy heads over to my parents and we just . . . hang out as a family."

"That's wonderful," this woman murmured, but the tone was off. And when he looked at her face, the pain in her eyes stole his breath. But then she was smiling, and it was gone—or maybe not gone so much as tucked carefully away.

"I'm sorry," she said with a sharp shake of her head. "I didn't even ask. How can I help you?"

Finn blinked, forced himself to focus on why he'd meandered over to this house in the first place, or at least on the reason he was telling himself he'd come over—that he most definitely *wasn't* lonely after having spent too much of the last years surrounded by people, but rather, was just trying to be a good neighbor. He held up the bucket inscribed with the name *Rylie* on it. "I found this on my deck. Wasn't sure if it had been misplaced or left behind, but I saw the toys on your deck and thought, perhaps, it might belong here."

"Left behind?"

"I'm renting the house next door." He pointed behind him to the small cottage that mirrored hers, one of a few houses lined up along the beach, their front doors facing the ocean. "Just for the summer." He waved the bucket slightly, the plastic shovel rattling. "I'm guessing there's only one Rylie in these parts."

"You've guessed right," she said, taking it from him, slipping beside him and out the front door to set it down in a large tub that held a gaggle of other beach toys. Less than a foot separated them, and he could smell the sweet floral notes of her hair, feel the heat of her body. Or maybe that was just him and more insanity.

He'd gone more than a year without feeling a lick of desire.

One glimpse of *this* woman, of her sad eyes, her sweet scent, and his cock twitched.

He wanted.

For the first time in as long as he could remember.

"Sorry it was left on your deck," she murmured, drawing him back into the conversation. "Rylie and the little girl who stayed there a few weeks earlier this summer were thick as thieves." Her mouth curved. "If you find any rogue toys, then *that* little one"—she pointed to her daughter, cuddled up with her stuffed animal, eyes on the page—"is probably the culprit."

Finn chuckled. "Noted. I'll be sure to storm over if I step on a Lego."

"Ah, you joke, but you must not have suffered that particular parental torture if you can make light of it." Her smile made his breath catch again.

She was . . . incredible.

Sweet. Lovely. Beautiful. And . . . sad.

So, *so* sad.

Her gaze met his, and he went rigid, hating the fact she was sad, this woman he didn't know from a stranger was in pain, and yet wondering how the rest of the world didn't see it, because otherwise they would want to storm in and take away that hurt.

But . . . he wasn't here for that.

He was messed up, and bringing his special brand of *messed up* into this woman's life wasn't an option. "I'm just going to go."

Sad got sadder.

And . . . *fuck*.

"Of course." She stepped back. "Thanks again."

Dark brown hair that shone in the afternoon sunlight, skin a deep gold that made the turquoise of her eyes stand out in sharp relief, lush, pink lips.

That parted.

That tipped up into a smile.

One that didn't reach her eyes. *Again.*

And even though he didn't know her, even though he was just going to be in town for a couple of months, *even though* she was only a temporary next-door neighbor—albeit one who seemed lovely and had an adorable kid—Finn made himself a promise.

In *that* moment, he made it his mission that if he did *nothing* else in his time away from Hollywood, then he would get this woman to smile for real.

Not just with her lips, but with her eyes.

With her heart.

He turned away, stopped, then spun back around to face her. "What's your name?"

"I'm Shannon," she murmured, extending a hand for him to shake.

His fingers met hers, his palm collided with hers, and . . . *sparks*, heat licking up his arm, consuming him with desire.

And Finn, who hadn't felt anything real in far too long—

His skin prickled, his cock twitched, and . . . his *heart* pulsed.

---

THANK YOU FOR READING! I hope you loved meeting Pepper and Derek! The next book in the Life Sucks series is Hot Mess. **He was the biggest movie star in the world, and quite possibly the only man whose life might be a bigger hot mess than her own. And...he wanted her.**

CLICK HERE TO READ HOT MESS NOW>

And if you enjoyed Train Wreck, you'll love the sexy, sweet, and close-knit Breakers Hockey crew. The first book in the series, BROKEN, is now live!

*It is sexy, hot, adorable and such a fun read. You will not be able to put this down!"* —Amazon Reviewer

Would you like to know about the disaster that happened at Christian Strand's house? Click here to sign up for my newsletter and to receive an exclusive bonus scene!

I so appreciate your help in spreading the word about my books, including sharing with friends! Please leave a review on your favorite book site!

You can also join my Facebook group, the Fabinators, for exclusive giveaways and sneak peeks of future books.

Hate missing Elise's new releases? Love contests, exclusive excerpts and giveaways?

Then signup for Elise's newsletter here!

https://www.elisefaber.com/newsletter

And join Elise's fan group, the Fabinators (https://www. facebook.com/groups/fabinators) for insider information, sneak peaks at new releases, and fun freebies! Hope to see you there!

LIFE SUCKS SERIES

*Life Sucks Series*
Train Wreck
Hot Mess
Dumpster Fire
Clusterf*@k
FUBAR
Perfect Storm
Free Fall

## ALSO BY ELISE FABER

### *Billionaire's Club* (all stand alone)

Bad Night Stand

Bad Breakup

Bad Husband

Bad Hookup

Bad Divorce

Bad Fiancé

Bad Boyfriend

Bad Blind Date

Bad Wedding

Bad Engagement

Bad Bridesmaid

Bad Swipe

Bad Girlfriend

Bad Best Friend

Bad Billionaire's Quickies

### *Gold Hockey* (all stand alone)

Blocked

Backhand

Boarding

Benched

Breakaway

Breakout

Checked

Coasting

Centered

Charging

Caged

Crashed

A Gold Christmas

Cycled

Caught

Cap

Covered

***Breakers Hockey (all stand alone)***

<u>Broken</u>

<u>Boldly</u>

<u>Breathless</u>

<u>Ballsy</u>

***Rush Hockey***

Big Puck Energy

Filthy Puckboy

So Pucking Over It

Love, Pucks, and Other Stories

***Love, Action, Camera (all stand alone)***

Dotted Line

Action Shot

Close-Up

End Scene

Meet Cute

## *Love After Midnight* (**all stand alone**)

Rum And Notes

Virgin Daiquiri

On The Rocks

Sex On The Seats

## *Life Sucks Series* (**all stand alone**)

Train Wreck

Hot Mess

Dumpster Fire

Clusterf*@k

FUBAR

## *Roosevelt Ranch Series* (**all stand alone, series complete**)

Disaster at Roosevelt Ranch

Heartbreak at Roosevelt Ranch

Collision at Roosevelt Ranch

Regret at Roosevelt Ranch

Desire at Roosevelt Ranch

## *Phoenix Series* (**read in order**)

Phoenix Rising

Dark Phoenix

Phoenix Freed

**Phoenix: *LexTal Chronicles* (rereleasing soon, stand alone, Phoenix world)**

From Ashes

In Flames

To Smoke

**KTS Series (all stand alone, series complete)**

Riding The Edge

Crossing The Line

Leveling The Field

Scorching The Earth

**Cocky Heroes World**

Tattooed Troublemaker

# ABOUT THE AUTHOR

*USA Today bestselling author*, Elise Faber, loves chocolate, Star Wars, Harry Potter, and hockey (the order depending on the day and how well her team -- the Sharks! -- are playing). She and her husband also play as much hockey as they can squeeze into their schedules, so much so that their typical date night is spent on the ice. Elise is the mom to two exuberant boys and lives in Northern California. Connect with her in her Facebook group, the Fabinators or find more information about her books at www.elisefaber.com.

f  facebook.com/elisefaberauthor

a  amazon.com/author/elisefaber

BB  bookbub.com/profile/elise-faber

  instagram.com/elisefaber

d  tiktok.com/@elisefaberauthor

g  goodreads.com/elisefaber

www.ingramcontent.com/pod-product-compliance
Lightning Source LLC
Chambersburg PA
CBHW022106240626

47153CB00007B/2261